CROSSFIELD
PUBLISHING

The Granby Liar

by Maurice J. O. Crossfield

A Novel

Crossfield, Maurice J.O. (1967-)

ISBN-13: 978-1-7751496-0-6 (Crossfield Publishing)

Cataloguing in Publication Data

Fiction, mystery, adult content

1. newspaper 2. Eastern Townships 3. Quebec 4. murder 5. intrigue 6. crime 7. politics

Cover artwork by Lawrence Stilwell

Interior layout by Harald Kunze

Manuscript prepared by Ernestine (Tina) Crossfield

Crossfield Publishing (since 1990), formerly located in Okotoks, Alberta, until 2013.

www.crossfieldpublishing.ca 1-226-301-4001

2269 Road 120, R7, St. Marys, Ontario, N4X 1C9, Canada

Publisher's note:

Maurice Crossfield and I are first cousins who are about 12 years of age apart, and for many years, separated by thousands of miles. We seldom crossed paths until 2010, when I was launching a new book in Montreal. Maurice and Sarah attended the event, and later in the evening, he mentioned to me that he had written a novel. Here we are 7 years later.

Createspace version   www.createspace.com

CROSSFIELD
PUBLISHING

Acknowledgements

The writing of this novel took place over several years, and as such requires the thanks of a number of people. Starting with my wife Sarah, whose grace and creativity never cease to inspire me. She's my true love, who's also pretty good at putting up with the neurotic behaviour of a tortured writer. Then there's Julien, who, should the beast be fully embraced, will be a better wordsmith than dad would ever hope to be. Brian Robinson, my guru, fitness coach and coffee philosopher. France Jodoin, who heads up my cheering section. Susan C. Mastine, who tackled the first round of editing. Susan Briscoe, whose love of prose and poetry inspired me to finally get this out into the world. And to Tina Crossfield, who I asked for some publishing advice, and after reading the manuscript said "I really want to publish this." My heartfelt thanks to you all.

And a special thanks to all of my former colleagues at The Sherbrooke Record, that mighty little paper that continues to be a vital thread in the fabric of the English-speaking community of the Eastern Townships.

***

Maurice J.O. Crossfield

Dedication

For my dad, John Crossfield (1936-1984)

What I wouldn't give to hear another story

Prologue

He was sweating even before the shovel hit the lid of the septic tank. It might have been a cold November night, but beads of sweat ran down his face, dripped off the end of his nose.

"Shit, shit, shit, shit," he mumbled to himself.

He'd been fine until he lost his temper. That's the problem when you carry a gun with you. Eventually you end up using it.

The shovel had no trouble getting through the frozen layer of topsoil. Then through the gravel that wouldn't freeze for another month yet. But when it hit the concrete lid it came to an abrupt halt.

A few more minutes of digging got him to the edge, and a few more after that he had cleared enough dirt away so that with a little leverage he could pry it open.

Bad enough that he shot the guy. Then he had a body to get rid of. He still had the dirt on him from the first hole, a place where it never would have been found. Until Rogers showed up. Everything went to hell from there. He wasn't about to shoot him too.

"One big cluster fuck," he mumbled to himself. For a man who spent his life keeping everything in his grasp under tight control, this wasn't working out.

It might have been cold out, but the contents of the septic tank were distinctly warm. A wave of warm, wet human waste cut his breath, and he had to stand back for a moment. He walked over to the parked Cadillac and reached for a bottle on the front seat that had no label on it. Old times.

But rather than take a drink to steady his nerves, he threw it back in the car. This was no moment for dull wits. He had to remain focused, not just on the job at hand, but on the bigger picture.

It's no easy task to move a body alone. But asking for help wasn't an option. It rolled out of the trunk and onto the ground with a quiet thump, and then he dragged it to the hole, hauling it by a short length of rope tied around the armpits. Leaning the torso over the edge of the hole, he pushed the body in head-first. "So you can see where you're going," he murmured.

A small plume of sewage splashed up onto his boot, making him step back in disgust. He got a rag from the trunk and wiped it off, throwing the rag into the septic tank where, with time, the bacteria would consume body, rag and any evidence that the cop ever existed.

There was going to be a lot of cleaning up to do.

1

I was just dozing off when the phone rang next to the bed.

"Dave Rogers?" the voice on the other end of the line asked.

"Yes."

"Harry Bankroft here. Listen, if you can get moved down here within two weeks the job is yours. The pay is bad, but we look the other way if you get the chance to freelance anything."

"Yeah, sure," I said, now fully awake. "I'll be there."

"Call the office tomorrow and ask for Linda. She'll be able to line you up with a place to stay and answer any questions you might have."

I looked at the clock. It was 10:30 p.m.

Ten days later I was in a picture postcard town, far different from the Montreal I'd known for the last 25 years. For the most part coming to Brigham was like stumbling into a Norman Rockwell painting, complete with general store, red brick United Church, and dirty little kid on a bicycle being followed by a dog.

The sun shone brightly in the typical Eastern Townships summer afternoon, leaving no doubt in anyone's mind that it was early July. The hazy humidity warned of a coming thunderstorm, and in a field across the river two men and a couple of teenagers were working frantically to get the rest of the hay in before the rain.

It was only an hour's drive from Montreal, but the surroundings were so different from anything I'd seen since I was a kid visiting my grandparents. Though I'd only been here for a day, I already felt the absence of the ambient noise, the energy of Montreal. It made me restless, and I hadn't slept worth a damn last night.

I reclined on the front porch of the two-bedroom bungalow I had rented with my wife and contemplated my new environment. A wind chime, left by the previous tenant, delicately sang with the breeze while underneath King, my German Shepherd mixed with God-knows-what, slept in the heat. Inside the house a mountain of boxes waited to be unpacked. But the heat commanded me to make them wait awhile longer.

Two weeks ago Jen, King and I had been living in a slightly rundown apartment in Notre Dame de Grace in Montreal. Okay, it was a dump.

Freshly out of McGill, I had sent out dozens of resume's to newspapers and magazines in the last couple of months, getting only the occasional "...unfortunately there are no positions open at this time..." letter. Or more often, no response at all.

Then, on June 10, 1975, I got a letter from the *Granby Leader-Mail*, a tiny newspaper that came out on Tuesdays and Fridays in the Eastern Townships. They needed a reporter, and liked the clippings I had sent them from my days at the McGill Daily News. Could I come in for an interview Wednesday?

A week later the phone call came, and my new career was launched. It was a job, and it wasn't like the big papers were exactly beating down my door. It wasn't my first choice, it was my only choice.

So it was off to the bush leagues, where I could spend time on my writing and be reasonably sure most of my stuff would get published. On the downside, I was also reasonably sure most of the news out here would be about little old ladies turning 100, and neighbors bitching about how each other's cows were in their flower beds. Still, I figured that with a little creativity I could make the stories interesting enough to write my way into the big leagues. Though I had been born in the Eastern Townships, we had moved to Montreal when I was a kid, leaving me with few memories of my birthplace, no attachment to the region or its people.

Leader-Mail reporters had been renting out the house in Brigham for years, and the previous tenant was the reporter I would be replacing. Despite a serious drinking problem he had managed to get an internship at Toronto's Globe and Mail, and wasn't looking back.

The lot backed onto the United Church, while the general store was only a couple hundred feet away. So was the only restaurant, local garage, post office, and pretty much everything else. When you move to a village of 200 people, nothing in town is ever very far. A number of locals driving by slowed down, probably to get a look at the new neighbour, I guessed. One guy, who I didn't get a good look at, brought his pickup truck to a full stop, chirping the tires as if in an expression of disgust as he pulled away. Others smiled politely and waved before continuing on their way.

In the distance an aging pale green Ford Falcon approached. It was Jen, back from a trip to Cowansville to pick up some groceries and a few other essentials. She had wound down all of the windows in an attempt to cool off, but as she stepped out of the car sweat glistened from her brow.

"Not much in the line of variety in the stores in Cowansville," she said, flapping her peasant dress with her free hand in the faint breeze. "But there's a hardware store there for when I put you to work fixing up this place."

Like all rented houses this one had become progressively run down over the years. The walls hadn't been painted since the Cuban Missile Crisis, and were covered in oily stains from a furnace that no longer worked like it was supposed to. Jennifer, my wife of two years, had it in her head that we were going to turn this grubby little dump into a home, just as she had with our last apartment in the city. She had an eye for decorating, and wasn't afraid to put me to work to make her vision see the light of day.

The house had two redeeming features: First the rent was cheap, and second... Well we couldn't think of a second redeeming quality just yet. I couldn't picture calling this place home at all.

But the heat took the edge off her drive to turn our new accommodations into a home. Instead she was content to join King and I on the porch. Fine woman that she was, she'd also picked up a case of beer on the way home, paid for with the tattered remnants of my student loan. With my salary as it was, this would be the last case for awhile.

At the Granby Leader-Mail reporters were required to have a university education. However the starting pay for a new reporter was minimum wage, or in the neighborhood of $140 a week. It was a salary job with no pay for overtime, though Bankroft would give you a little extra time off if you'd worked exceptionally hard. My work hours would depend on the assignments, and I was also in a weekend rotation with the other reporters, working one out of every four. Two weekends on duty was rewarded with four days off.

"I called the library in Cowansville, and they said there might be an opening in a couple of weeks," Jen said as she dropped into an aluminum lawn chair. "One of the librarians is pregnant, and she's having a hard time of it."

Jen was looking for anything to help us make a few extra bucks, and she particularly loved books. I met her when she was working part time at the library at McGill, as a matter of fact. I knew she'd rather be home doing her pottery, but right now there wasn't a whole lot of choice in the matter.

That night it took me hours to get to sleep, a combination of the heat and the sheer dread of starting a new job tomorrow. I'd dreamed of my first newspaper job for years now, and my dreams hadn't looked anything like the brief glimpse of the Granby Leader-Mail I'd seen at the interview. My mind raced with imagined arguments with fellow reporters and angry phone calls from people I'd blown the whistle on. I pushed aside the thoughts that all I really wanted was to go home.

By about 4 a.m. I finally began to lose consciousness. As I did so I faintly remember hearing the thunder in the distance, the inevitable storm that would finally break the week-long heat wave.

***

In my dream my father is sitting at the kitchen table, a cup of coffee at one hand, a cigarette clenched between the scarred fingertips of the other. He fills the room. He seems lost in thought as I make my way around him to the sink.

"Why would you want to work out there?" he asks.

"I need a job."

"But why out there? There's nothing out there. Small little paper that gets it wrong more often than not. Won't do you any good. You had a perfectly good job at the garage."

"Like I said dad, I need a job, and not fixing cars. It's just until I get some experience, then Jen and I are going to move on."

"There's nothing out there for you anymore. It's all gone."

"What's all gone?"

"Everything."

"I'm not looking for anything."

"You don't have to be looking. There's nothing there that's good for you. You should pack up and move elsewhere."

"You've said that before. What are you on about?"

"You should be more than this."

"I am more than this. Not that you were ever around to find out."

"You make it sound like I had a choice."

"It's not like you gave me much for choices."

"I didn't get to decide that. You know that as well as I do. You need to start listening."

"Dad, what in the hell are you talking about?"

And then the mechanical grind of the electric alarm clock shattered my sleep, rousing me for my first day of work.

2

The offices of the Granby Leader-Mail were set up at the intersection of Mountain and Drummond Streets, right in the core of Granby. With a population of about 25,000, Granby could have been considered a large town or a small city, depending on where you came from.

While Granby was the largest town in the region covered by the Leader-Mail, the focus of the paper was increasingly on the smaller towns. In 1975 the English had begun leaving Quebec, scared off by the October Crisis in 1970, the continuing rise of separatism and the general feeling they didn't belong anymore. Granby was primarily French, while the English speakers that remained lived mainly in towns to the south, like East Farnham, Cowansville, Knowlton, Sutton and any number of smaller hamlets that dotted the countryside. With the numbers of English speakers declining, many learned French to make life easier. Most of the time everybody got along in whatever language worked best, despite the best efforts of the political class.

The Leader-Mail building had served many functions over the years, first as a small furniture plant, and later as a tent factory. About 20 years earlier the paper moved into the two-storey brick building, which still had the same dirty windows covered with steel mesh that had been bolted there five decades before. They were too high and too dirty to look out of, yellowed by years of cigarette smoke, furnace oil and paper dust.

Inside the paper's offices were set up in what looked like a warehouse, with the administration, advertising and newsroom filling up the space. Just a few years ago they finally walled off the print shop so the office workers could still hear the phones during the press runs. The presses ran more regularly these days, as the company resorted to printing advertising flyers to make ends meet.

Harry Bankroft was in every day by noon, and usually worked until 10 or 11 p.m. every night. Though he ate enough greasy food to kill two people, a high metabolism kept his 45-year-old five-foot-ten birdlike frame from ever tipping the scales over 140 pounds. His high strung nature also ensured he avoided sitting still, except when he was writing stories, editing the latest efforts of the four reporters, or figuring out how the pages were going to be pasted together.

Bankroft thrived on the pressure, usually leaving as much work as possible until the final couple of hours before press time. A former copy editor at The Montreal Star, he missed the daily thrill of getting the paper out on time. But twice a week he got that old feeling, occasionally followed by a few bolts of lightning in his left arm and some shortness of breath.

Everyone in the newsroom smoked, and Bankroft was no exception. He never lit up during the day. Instead his habit kicked in when it came time to write or edit copy. He would then sit down, open a fresh pack of Export A greens, remove the foil, and chain smoke. When the first pack was done a second one was opened, and another dozen cigarettes were consumed one by one. He never used more than two matches a day, lighting one off the other.

Part of Bankroft's personal mission for the paper was to wipe out the nickname given it by the locals over the years. For many it was better known as the "Granby Liar," due in large part to several high profile lawsuits, which the paper fought and lost. Those losses nearly sealed the paper's fate.

Over the last several years Bankroft had looked long and hard for talented writers with a commitment to solid reporting. The problem was the really good ones were eventually called into the big leagues, wooed by large salaries and the chance to rise to the top of their profession. The Granby Liar was left with what it could afford, a collection of new people and veterans with few prospects.

When Bankroft first saw Dave Rogers' clippings, he detected potential. There was a crispness in his prose, a glimmer of talent. Sure, he wrote like a college boy, but that was unavoidable after four years of university life. Bankroft would soon break him of that, cut his vocabulary and his attitude down to size.

When Dave arrived for his interview Harry was in the middle of writing a cop short about a break-and-enter in Roxton, one of the two dozen or so towns covered by the paper. Rogers was made to wait on a battered, low-slung couch nearby, shifting uncomfortably in his new suit.

When Bankroft turned to look down at him he saw someone who looked much like any other brown nosing wannabe reporter. The short blond hair had been freshly cut for the job hunt, and the cheap suit didn't quite fit properly over the six-foot frame.

"So you must be Davis," Bankroft had said.

"Rogers, sir. Dave Rogers."

"Sorry, you looked a bit like this Davis guy I recently did a piece about. Bad cat, likes to get drunk and beat up people, a real wahoo," Bankroft went on. "Hope no one around here mistakes him for you, or you might get your head busted. His is too hard to break."

During the interview Bankroft got the information he needed, using the short, sharp questions that had become his trademark over the last two decades in journalism. Rogers was 29, born in the Townships but moved to the city at age five when dad suddenly decided he didn't want the family farm. He died shortly after. Dave Jr. Graduated high school, then spent the next five years working as busboy, gas station attendant and finally as an apprentice mechanic. Then it was off to university where he met his wife of the last six months. Graduated solidly in the middle of his class, lived in NDG, needed a job. No kids. Surprisingly confident for someone seemingly desperate for a break.

Bankroft hired Rogers for three main reasons: First, he had scratched out a living in the real world, so he could identify with the workies who made up the bulk of the readership. Second, he seemed to be able to think on his feet, an important quality in a business where screwing up was at times a way of life. Thirdly, he seemed to be able to write passably well.

After he called Dave up to let him know he was hired and where there was a cheap place for rent, he didn't give him a second thought. Until Harry arrived at the office a couple of weeks later and there was this guy again, complete with shirt and tie, wandering around aimlessly. Probably the only reporter with a tie to work here in years, he thought.

"You a reporter or a lawyer?" Bankroft asked.

"I thought this was a TV job," replied Dave.

"Ever been to court?"

"No."

"Well you'd better get your ass down there. The cops have arrested a guy for stealing cows, and he's going to be charged this afternoon."

"How do I know who he is?" Dave asked.

"Go to the front and ask for the clerk. She should be able to point you in the right direction. While you're there, keep your eyes open for this short fat cop named Dubois. He handles the media and is sure to be there with the details of how they used all of their crime fighting skills to trap this criminal genius with a taste for beef."

With that Dave was sent off to launch a career that would begin with a cattle thief.

3

So here I was, sitting in the office at the Granby Leader-Mail, wondering what I should do next. I had reported for work at ten, and when I showed up there was only one reporter there. He introduced himself as John McAuslan, welcomed me to the paper and then rushed out the door.

Linda, the newsroom secretary, had met me when I came in. She said Bankroft hadn't given her any instructions as to what I was supposed to be doing or where. She introduced me to the vacant desk which she figured was the one intended for me. So I sat there, first reading the most recent edition of the paper, then moving on to the other newspapers stacked in the corner. To keep up with things newspaper offices usually subscribe to any others they can get their hands on, so there's never a shortage of reading material.

Pausing from my reading to look around, I was taken in once again by how this didn't look like what I thought my first office would look like. It looked like a newsroom in a 1940's film noir, after a bomb had gone off on the set. Everyone seemed to smoke, and the building had apparently been erected with no mind for ventilation. Luckily last night's storm had killed the heat and humidity, but a constant blue haze hung in the room.

George Brown was the publisher of the Granby Leader-Mail. This short fat man smoked particularly vile smelling cigars. I think they were White Owl's, the type my mom threatened to force me to smoke if she ever caught me with a cigarette. As he was walking by Linda stopped him to introduce him to his newest underling.

"Welcome to the Granby Liar," he grunted in a voice filled with gravel. He turned his back and walked away before I could say anything.

Tiring of both my reading and my warm reception, I began wandering the building. The people in advertising visited amongst themselves, and totally ignored my existence. I wondered how they ever managed to sell much of anything with all that gossiping going on. But salespeople are by nature the most social of beings, and stopping them from talking would be like trying to stop a tidal wave with a dinner fork.

In production, four people were working over light tables, pasting up the comics, death notices and some of the social notes. This was where the paper took shape, put together with skilled hands, wax and knives. These guys were so much faster than anything I'd ever managed to do pasting up the *McGill Daily News*. The end product was a lot cleaner looking too.

As I was wandering back to my desk, in walks Harry Bankroft. He isn't there 20 seconds and he's already sending me on my first assignment, something to do with a cattle thief. My first vision was of some guy stuffing a cow into a Volkswagen Beetle in the middle of the night, and I had a hard time not to smile. Mind you the prospect of covering court as my very first assignment did a lot to help me take things seriously. I'd never seen the inside of a courtroom except on a black and white TV, not in real life Technicolor. I was being thrown to the wolves and I hadn't even collected my first paycheque yet.

I pictured the headline: Fledgling Reporter Freaks Out, Skips Town. At that moment it seemed like the sensible option.

Fortunately I have a talent for looking calm when I'm actually about to soil myself. It helped during the job interview, and I was sure it would come in handy from time to time at my new job. I didn't say a word, picked up my note pad, and headed out the door.

Pity I didn't ask directions to the courthouse.

Too embarrassed to go back and ask, I drove to the nearest phone booth and looked up the address. Then I drove back to the parking lot at the Leader-Mail, walked across the street, down two buildings and into the courthouse. So much for claiming mileage.

The courthouse was a dumpy little building, which, as I learned later, the government was already planning to replace. Inside the dumpy little building I found a dumpy little clerk who without so much as a word, pointed me to dumpy little courtroom B.

They're in the middle of going through the roll, and my cattle rustler is in there somewhere. The process is so fast the prosecutors don't even read out the charges, giving the numbers in the criminal code instead. The sickening feeling that I'm going to come up empty on my first assignment returns.

Then this extremely dirty little guy appears at the dock in hand cuffs. I glance at his work boots and spot what I think is cow shit. I'm no expert in the matter, but a few seconds later I get a faint whiff, and I know I've got my man.

The feeling of confidence vanishes abruptly once again when, before anything seems to happen, the judge orders the man to return for a bail hearing in two days.

At that moment I see the fat little cop Bankroft was talking about get up and leave the courtroom. I get up and give chase.

Fernand Dubois was a provincial cop for fifteen years before he was sidelined by heart problems. After that he was reassigned to a desk, ending up being the unofficial flak who deals with reporters questions so the healthy cops can continue to beat up the bad guys. He likes being recognized as the man in charge, even though they don't even give him a gun anymore.

Following a brief introduction, Dubois launches into a speech, giving me the information I need, including a rundown of just what it was I'd seen in the courtroom.

"His name is Mark Simson, age 22. For the last six months he has been stealing cattle across the region, from Dunham to Shefford Township. The first theft took place in April, and the last one happened last night. In between we believe he has been involved in no less than ten thefts, stealing a total of 25 cattle."

After a brief pause, "He used a horse trailer pulled behind a truck, which was reported stolen during the winter. We also believe there were two other men involved in the thefts, and we are expecting to make further arrests as the investigation progresses."

"What did he do with the stolen cattle?" I asked, my absurd imagination conjuring up images of cattle sold into slavery. Cutting sugar cane, probably.

"The cattle, we believe, were then sold to a slaughterhouse somewhere outside the region. It appears our cow thief and his friends were part of a bigger operation."

He then changed the subject, filling me in on the charges (25 counts of cattle theft), the names of the lawyers and the judge involved, and when the smelly little bugger would be back in front of a judge.

By the time I got back to the office the other reporters had returned from their various assignments. John McAuslan I'd met before, and this time he was too busy to say much. Then there was Rachel Porter, the first and only female reporter on staff, and Steve Farnham. The introductions were brief and friendly, and for the first time I felt welcomed to this warehouse of words. Too bad I still didn't feel like a reporter.

Over the next hour I banged away at an ancient Underwood typewriter, turning out my debut at the Granby Leader-Mail. Bankroft then tore it to pieces with a pencil while I looked over his shoulder, pulling out words, moving quotes and making it clear that Simson was accused of crimes, but not convicted. "On the night of March 15 Simson allegedly drove to a field on 10th Range Road in Dunham where police say he stole three cows..." and so on.

Upon questioning I admitted I didn't know what kind of cattle they were. They have different kinds?

Bankroft said nothing further to me about the story. He didn't say it was bad, didn't say it was good. Didn't offer any advice, just sat there and smoked. As I looked around plumes of smoke rose from behind the other typewriters as words spilled onto pages and lives changed all around us.

4

The next few days were a little easier on me as I got into the swing of things at The Granby Liar. I left the suit at home, opting instead for jeans and a decent shirt. I didn't go back to the courthouse for the bail hearing, but followed it up by phone instead. That happens a lot when you're busy and you figure there isn't much to be gained by going in person.

The next half dozen assignments were in fact more along the lines of what I had expected. Being the new guy I ended up as the one sent to the 103rd birthday party, and to a farm to do a story on a prize Holstein. The guy who didn't even realize cows came in different breeds was writing a story about what constituted a champion. That happens a lot in journalism. More than most of us would care to admit.

I was also sent to a number of press conferences. These ranged in subject matter from political issues to company openings to social groups asking for more funding and so on. It wasn't exactly exciting news like a shooting or a robbery, but Bankroft reminded me that it was still stuff that affected the lives of our readers. So I turned it out.

One of the things I noticed about these press conferences was that almost all of the same people went to all of them. At the mayor's press conference on the future of the hospital the local Member of Parliament was there, along with the head of the chamber of commerce. At the MP's press conference on housing the mayor was there, joined by the head of the chamber of commerce. When the chamber held its own press conference on the need to attract new investment to the region, the MP and the mayor were in the audience.

The only thing that seemed to change was the seating arrangement. Even the rhetoric was similar, and with the exception of a few facts and figures you could pretty much tell what they were going to say: The mayor wanted the hospital to stay, the MP wanted more housing, and the chamber prez wanted more people to invest.

Each of these press conferences turned into 15-inch stories that ended up on page four or five. The finished product usually looked like what I wrote, though maybe a little better, I reluctantly had to admit.

Perhaps I'll give you a little rundown of how these press conferences ended up on the printed pages of nearly 8,000 copies of the Leader-Mail every Tuesday and Friday. From the depths of my consciousness to the bottom of your birdcage, so to speak.

My stuff came out of an old manual Underwood that looked like something from an army surplus store. Fellow reporter Rachel Porter and Bankroft were kitted out with new IBM Selectrics, while the rest of us pounded away on the older manual machines. Every story was done with a carbon copy, just in case. Reporters being what they are, most of the writing was done on Mondays and Thursdays, at the last possible minute.

From there Bankroft would edit the latest offerings with a pencil for the minor changes, and with scissors and paste for the big things, like moving paragraphs.

"When the final copy looks pretty much like your carbon copy, then you'll know you've made the grade," he said on my second day on the job. Nothing more was said about if I was doing my job properly or not. That feeling of uncertainty would be my constant companion in those early weeks, fading away only gradually. Honestly, it never really goes away.

From there the story was sent to the typists, who entered the corrected versions into two machines, each about the size of an upright grand piano. Both typists were practically blind from years of squinting into the tiny screens, which showed only the last dozen characters entered.

That machine in turn produced a ticker tape, which was then fed into an optical reader. This reader burned the letters onto light sensitive paper, much like when you develop a photograph.

Once this paper was developed - in a machine about the size of a Volkswagen van - and dried, it was then cut into strips for paste-up.

At the light tables these long strips of text were then cut and pasted into place, as directed by layout sheets Bankroft drew up with a ruler and pencil. Car theft story over three columns, light headline. Photo on right centre with provincial budget story on its left, bold headline with a light kicker above the fold. And on it went, page after page. Local news, provincial and national, then editorial. Social notes, pages of them, then death notices, comics and on the back pages, sports. Entertainment news, including the TV listings, came out in a separate section every Friday.

Usually, after all the copy had gone out and was waiting its turn at the light tables, Bankroft would wander around, barking orders, smoking, and on Monday and Thursday nights especially, rubbing his chest.

Those pasted together pages were then sent to the print shop in back, where they were photographed and the printing plates were made. Two hours later, at about 1 a.m., the papers were loaded into the trucks and on their way to the corner stores and post offices. By noon those who subscribed had the paper on their doorstep on in their mailbox.

Considering the process involved, no one ever yelled to stop the presses. That only happened in movies. Here, if you got that interview a little too late, you missed the boat. Bankroft ran hot and cold on these things, so you never knew if you were going to get in shit for it or not.

In the first couple of months all new reporters become workaholics, desperate to prove themselves, prove they deserve the job. Though only paid for eight hours a day, I worked ten and 12 hours, the air of uncertainty always looking over my shoulder. The lack of any kind of feedback from the boss fed the air of uncertainty, made me push even harder. But in those early days the exciting stories eluded me.

Usually I went home only to slip into the sheets next to my sleeping wife. After the first few times Jen didn't even wake up anymore. I, on the other hand, would toss and turn for a couple of hours before falling into a fitful slumber. Four or five hours later I was up and around, getting ready to go back to work.

Most of my conversations with Jen took place on the phone from work, avoiding the real emerging issues between us in favour of reporting to each other what we had done during the day.

Things hadn't been nearly as exciting in this new life for her. The library job hadn't worked out yet, and we didn't have the cash to set up the house. Any spare money went into the Ford Falcon, which I needed for work, and which was starting to develop some bad personality traits. Most days Jen was home alone with the dog, in a tiny rundown house in a tiny rundown town, and no game plan of her own.

I finally realized there was a serious problem when I came home one evening and she was standing on the porch with her bags packed one evening in late July.

"Going somewhere?" I asked in a light tone of voice while my stomach began churning and my mouth went dry.

"I have to get out of this place," came the curt reply.

"What's wrong?"

"Everything. You, this town, this shack we live in, I can't handle it. I went to university for four years and here I sit, housebound and married to a man I never see anymore. When you are here you're not really here, you're thinking about work."

I won't go into the details, except to say that the next four hours brought the both of us through the full range of emotions. First I was mad, screaming about how all I was trying to do was be a success. Then she was mad, saying I didn't seem to care about anything else. At one point she was leaving, then I was leaving. We fought, we cried, we held each other.

That night we both collapsed into each other's arms, exhausted from the battle. No love making, just promises to protect one another from the rest of the world. Promises from me not to let my work dominate our lives.

The next morning I put her on the bus for Montreal. She needed time with friends, family and familiar surroundings, while I had my first turn at the weekend shift.

5

Over the next few weeks I finally began settling in to my new job and my new surroundings. It would be some time however before I figured out how to balance work and the rest of my life, and it would be a lie to say that the fight with Jen was the last. Couples tend to fight over reoccurring issues, and hopefully they eventually learn from their mistakes before it's too late.

Being a small town reporter brings with it a certain celebrity status that goes beyond what's really deserved. In the city papers most people don't even take notice of who writes the stories. But I quickly learned that out here in the country the locals read every printed word, even the bylines and the photo credits.

Some people, upon learning that they're in the presence of a reporter, get self-conscious, punctuating their conversations with comments like "Don't print that!", or "I hope this doesn't end up in the paper." It's as if they think I'm taking copious notes when they're not looking, preparing for an exposé on their comments about life, religion, politics and that the neighbour thinks the minister has a drinking problem.

But not everyone was enamored with the Granby Leader-Mail or its scribes. One day I was having lunch with Jen at a Cowansville coffee shop when this short, stocky, filthy man in a plaid shirt walks up to my table. He has what appears to be one thick, black eyebrow.

"You the new guy at the Granby Liar?" he asked, with just the slightest hint of contempt in his voice.

"Yes."

"You might want to get yerself a real job there, boy."

"Oh really," I replied, caught a little off guard by this unexpected attack. I really couldn't think of anything else to say. I noticed that the other conversations in the coffee shop had come to an abrupt halt.

"You just better watch what you're writin' about, cause if you piss off the wrong folks you won't last long."

"Can I quote you on that?" I replied in attempt to get some of my own back.

"Take it to the bank, Rogers."

With that the filthy man with the one eyebrow walked out of the coffee shop and stepped into a shiny new GMC pickup. A passing car came to a halt to let him pull out onto the street.

"Looks like you've met the president of your fan club," Jen said.

"I bet the eyebrow helps keep the water out of his eyes in the shower," I said.

"That would imply the man actually showers."

It didn't take long before I had passed off this little encounter. Though newspapers are supposed to sell, being a reporter can't always be a popularity contest. People get mad when you pry into their affairs, but they're the same people to scream if they don't get to read the dirt on everyone else.

Personally I kind of enjoyed cheesing people off. To me it meant they were reading my stories and reacting to them. It was especially pleasing when you know they damn well deserved to look bad. Just make sure you've got your facts straight, and let the chips fall where they may.

One day I did a piece on a guy who had been selling pot, hash and speed to high school kids through his 15 year old son. Known locally as Paul Pot, the guy had been making a small killing off of teenagers who were spending their lunch money on the stuff.

The cops sent a narc onto the school bus. A 19 year old cop in training who looked 15. He got close to the boy, and in a matter of a few days scored a dime bag of weed and three hits of speed. The next day father and son are hauled off to the courthouse.

I wasn't around when Paul Pot and Junior were busted. But I was there when, six months later, daddy's day in court came along. I was also there the following week for the sentencing.

It seems that Paul Pot got his son to take the fall for him. The son said he'd stolen the dope from daddy, all on his own. Dad got a six-month suspended sentence while the boy was sent to the Shawbridge Boys Farm for four months.

I guess I was a little irked by this guy who would get his kid to take the fall, and it showed in the story I wrote. Reporters are supposed to be impartial observers of these things. Bankroft, perhaps feeling the same disgust as I was, ran my story with only a few minor changes, my point of view coming out loud and clear.

The day after the story appeared Paul Pot got my home phone number. He screamed at me for about five minutes straight, which gave me enough time to gather my forces and get ready to scream back. The conversation was colourful and to the point. It came to a sudden halt when I told him that I knew a cop who owed me a favour, and if he ever called me again I'd see that his suspended sentence turned into jail time.

"You're full of shit," he said, and hung up.

He was right, of course. But the ploy worked. He never called me again, never carried out the threats he made. When I saw him at the grocery store a few weeks later he ignored me. Judging from the red-rimmed eyes, I suspect he didn't even remember what I looked like, though I know he had seen me taking notes in the courtroom. That whole note-taking thing tends to make you stand out in a crowd.

A few days later, while having an after work beer with my fellow reporters, they reinforced what I already believed: These guys never live up to their threats. They kick and scream, but that's about it. The more intelligent ones eventually realize that it's all part of the game, and work harder not to be tripped up the next time. Most career criminals and some politicians never get it right, giving reporters plenty to do, even in small towns.

In the process they also learn one of the beauties of reporting: I always get the last word. Just like now.

Those early weeks at the Granby Liar also saw the formation of lifelong friendships with my coworkers. Rachel Porter was high strung and hard nosed, much in the tradition of Harry Bankroft. While she was more approachable, she was never at a loss to point out the errors in my writing style. It was done without malice, but rather a blunt sense of honesty she just couldn't suppress. John McAuslan had been at the paper for three years and was burned out by the journalism game. He wanted to do something else, but until he figured out what that was, he was staying put. Steve Farnham took nothing seriously, except for the high school hockey games and basketball tournaments he covered for the sports pages.

Through our discussions at work and at the Barrel, a local tavern noted for its 30 cent draft, I began to learn more about the region and its people. For the most part they were hard working blue collar types, filling factories in towns like Granby, Cowansville and Waterloo. Others lived off the land, just as their families had done for generations. Though I first saw them as unsophisticated hicks, I slowly began to realize that it wasn't a lack of intelligence but rather that they had knowledge of different things. Things that I knew nothing about but they needed to know to survive. I knew how to flag down a cab or fend off a panhandler, while they knew when it was time to put the corn in or how to drop a tree without getting yourself killed.

The biggest bonus of my new job was the time on the road. Reporters get around a lot, and the scenery in the Townships was even more beautiful than what I remembered as a kid. Ancient maples formed a canopy over country lanes lined with stone walls, whispering memories to each other in hushed tones, in case the sun might overhear. Tones that touched you inside before vanishing into the ether, never to be heard again, their exact form impossible to remember.

Those times on the road are remembered as some of the most relaxing I've ever had. No one could reach me by phone as I cruised along in the Falcon. Once or twice I pulled over, only to perch for a few moments on a stone wall or eat my lunch on the roadside while listening to the radio.

Jen also began to settle into life in the country. The library job finally came up, and she had work four days a week. She also began making friends with the neighbors, and started taking classes with a local weavers guild.

I came home one day to discover the basement had been turned into a pottery studio. She was up to her elbows in clay, and had the largest smile on her face I'd seen in weeks. It was accompanied by a light in her eyes that she gets when she's in the midst of a creative rush. It's a look that never fails to turn me on, even though I know I could never coax her into the bedroom when she's like that.

"What's going on here?" I asked as I stepped down the stairs into the basement. King was lying nearby, having discovered that the basement was an excellent spot to escape the heat and humidity of early August.

"I was at the weaver's guild today and I met this woman named Carol Ann. We got to talking and it turns out pottery used to be a bit of an obsession of hers. But her asthma got in the way," she was talking fast, almost frantic. "She gave me this wheel, some leftover clay and a few other doodads."

"What, no kiln?" I asked jokingly, glancing around the basement to see if she hadn't somehow managed to miraculously drag one down the stairs while I was gone.

"That's the best part. Her husband has a one-ton truck. He's going to bring it over Saturday, so you'll have to be here to figure out how to unload the thing."

So there I was, two days later, in the middle of yet another heat wave, inching an 800 pound kiln off of a truck with a guy named George. Somehow we managed to get it set up in a corner of the yard. Making it operational was going to be another thing altogether.

"Your problem now," he said with a smile as he pulled out of the driveway.

6

"Stubby Booker made me do it!"

The comment jolted me back to attention. Suddenly, I had a whole new ball game on my hands.

I had spent most of the day in the Granby courthouse, in part to cover Mark Simson, the cow thief who marked my grand entry to the wild world of small town journalism just over a month ago. It had been a long day, and I hadn't entirely been paying attention.

Simson had been released on bail three days after his arrest in July. Two weeks later he got into a fight at Lucky's Tavern and went back into the slam. At a routine court appearance two weeks ago he pleaded guilty to all charges. We had missed that little surprise.

Today it was sentencing time. For two hours in the morning I had been listening as the Crown Prosecutor went chapter and verse through Simson's previous criminal record, then moved on to similar cases in which heavy sentences were handed down. The prosecutor, a hawkish looking man named Johnson, wanted our cow thief to get a minimum of four years in a federal jail.

Simson's lawyer was equally exciting. A little tiny man named Hermanson, he went through the parts of his client's life that Johnson had ignored in the afternoon: He came from a broken home, his father used to beat him, it sucked to be Mark Simson. If you were him you would have stolen cows too. Hermanson was calling for three year's probation, nothing more, and cited his own selection of previous cases in which people like Simson were allowed to walk.

Then came an hour's break while judge Martin decided Simson's fate. That time was spent hanging around in the hallways of the courthouse, looking at old photos of judges and lawyers, members of the local bar association. If I had smoked it would have at least given me something to do. Something to help me fit in with the others.

When judge Martin returned to the courtroom it was to side largely with Johnson. After running down some of the facts of the case, he gave Simson a sentence of three years, to be served in a federal jail.

"Stubby Booker made me do it!" Simson blurted out "I had no choice, it wasn't up to me!"

31

Simson was frantic, looking about the room like a caged animal. He took a step towards the judge and two guards grabbed him, setting off a rattle of leg irons and handcuffs. The struggle was brief, and Simson realized that his fate was sealed.

"Anything you say now will have no influence on your sentence," Martin said. "Do you have anything else to say?"

Simson went silent and looked at his feet. He shook his head.

I was scribbling furiously now, more awake than I had been all day. Most of the time not much happens in court, but when things start to move they move fast.

As the judge left the courtroom I rushed to the prisoner's dock to see if I could get anything more, joined by a reporter from the local AM station. I asked Simson if he had anything else to say.

"No, I have nothing to say. Please don't print anything," he said, the caged animal look returning. "I never said that."

He turned his back and the guards led him away. Next stop: Club Fed.

From there it was back to the office. It was Monday afternoon, and I had a deadline to meet. I also had three stories to write.

When I got back to the office I saw that my coworkers were all up against the same deadline, smoking furiously and writing fast. Bankroft paused briefly to ask how court had gone.

"Not bad at all. Simson got three years, and then blurted out that some guy named Booker made him do it."

Bankroft's eyes lit up.

"Stubby Booker?"

"Yeah, that's the guy. Is he anyone special?"

"He's our local crime boss," chirped in Rachel from a blue cloud behind her Selectric. "Serious bad boy."

"Oh, really," I said, feeling a sudden rush. This story was getting better all the time. I was about to press for a few more details on our small town hood when Bankroft cut me off.

"Get your ass in gear and get writing. There'll be plenty of time later to talk about this."

So it was off to my Underwood. I warmed up with my story on the new X-ray machine at the hospital. From there I wrote the Mark Simson court story, complete with the "Stubby Booker made me do it!" quote near the top. I wrapped up my writing three hours after I had begun with a piece on a Hydro plan to move a substation to a farm outside of Granby.

After work I met up with Rachel Porter and John McAuslan. Bankroft was still at the office, chain smoking and dissecting our stories. He'd call us at The Barrel if he had any questions.

The Barrel was a dirty, run down place not far from the office. There were a half dozen regulars who showed up in the afternoon every day and stayed until closing, watching baseball in the summer and hockey in the winter. In between they watched football, golf or reruns of Hogan's Heroes. English or French depended on who was working, or if there was a patron with a bit of a mood on.

After ordering up a pitcher of draft I asked the question that had been nagging at me since my coworkers had taken a sudden interest in my cow thief story.

"So who in hell is Stubby Booker?" I asked.

Rachel looked carefully around to see if anyone had overheard before beginning her narrative. She picked this up from an old woman she met while on assignment who was a neighbor of the Booker clan.

***

"Stubby, aka Sanford Booker, was born into a dirt poor family in Roxton Pond during the Depression. In the early years he was beaten, along with his mother, by a father who came back messed up from the first war. Unable to hold anything other than a bottle daddy Booker was pretty much a complete screw up, and seemed intent on dragging Stubby and his mom along for the ride. Most people were poor in the Depression, but the Booker household was the lowest of the low. Almost no one ever helped them because everyone was afraid of Stubby's dad.

One day when Sanford was at the tender age of five, his dad, in a drunken rage, decided to cut off the end of his kid's thumb, apparently in some attempt to show him how painful life can be. Sanford, who in the coming years would become known as Stubby, ran to the neighbour's.

The next day Stubby comes home to find his mother beaten to death and his dad swinging from a rafter in the attic. An orphan at the age of five who only ever knew about abuse, Stubby ended up being raised by his maternal grandmother.

Stubby's granny raised her grandson by strict rules, never hesitating to bring out the strap if he got out of line. He was an angel at home, but a hellion out in the world. And if anyone ever questioned Stubby's actions, granny was there, ready to take on anyone who had a cross word about her grandson, deserved or not.

As the Johnny Cash song goes, he grew up fast and he grew up mean. He was always spoiling for a fight, and by the age of ten seemed to be fueled by little more than a smoldering rage. Maybe because of his dad. Maybe because he's just a prick.

By the age of 15 he began his life of crime, smuggling booze across the border. At first he carried the stuff across through the woods, then he discovered the dozens of unmarked border crossings around here. He stole a car from Montreal and began making real money, branching out later into contraband tobacco and anything else that could be hauled across the border for profit.

Granny stood by him, ready to take on anyone who questioned Stubby's story that he worked at a furniture plant in Cowansville. Once, so the story goes, she took a swing at a cop who showed up to ask her some questions about the boy.

By the age of 20 Stubby heads up a crew of five dragging anything across the border they can make a buck at. The stolen car was replaced by old trucks, and later, new ones. Booze was the number one commodity, though there is some speculation he was one of the first around here to see the benefits of smuggling pot to the States.

A few years later Stubby was emerging as a force to be reckoned with. Some other bad cats began giving him a hard time, even trying to kill him once. One of them disappeared, never to be heard from again, while another was missing for almost ten years before his body was found in a quarry in Bedford.

By the time he was looking 30 in the eye, Stubby shot Marty Martin, the guy everyone believed was his boss. Booker was arrested, but because the cops were still pissed about never being able to jail Martin, they don't work too hard at it. Stubby, armed with a good lawyer and a bag full of cash, walks.

From what we can tell, by this time Booker is the undisputed crime boss in the Townships. He's got his fingers in more pies and a bunch of cops on the payroll. Then he pushes a little to far and shoots a cop in a fit of rage. This should have sunk him. But Stubby always thinks on his feet. Where the cop's body goes is anybody's guess, but it's never been found.

Of course Booker now has every cop on his ass big time. They're nailing his trucks, raiding his house and turning the Townships upside down looking for a corpse. They even get a guy who's prepared to testify against Stubby, says he saw the whole thing.

But no body means no murder charge, and with some wrangling Stubby gets two years in the slam for obstruction of justice. It's the only jail time he ever serves. In that time the witness to the cop killing disappears.

Today local lore has it Stubby Booker has his hand in almost everything, from strip bars to stolen cars to growing dope. I once heard from a guy in a bar that Stubby hires the real wizards in the pot businesses, the ones into the real scientific end of things, getting the biggest buzz for your buck. If someone gets busted, chances are they aren't one of his growers, or if they are there's no way it can be proven. In fact most of it is hard to prove. One thing's for sure, most people around here are terrified of him."

And now I was scared too.

7

Rachel and John, seeing the look of concern on my face, reassured me that Stubby liked the attention of being the celebrity criminal, a sort of small town Al Capone. They fed me a couple of extra Molson Exports to cheer me up.

Nevertheless, the discovery that I was dragging a dangerous man into a story that he might not like being part of kind of bothered me. On the way home along the Adamsville Road I spent a lot of time looking in the rear-view mirror of the Falcon, even though there was no way for Stubby to have read the story yet.

To take my mind off of things I turned on the AM radio. The Granby station ran rock and roll late at night, the kind of music that the hippies all loved at McGill. I loved it too, even though I didn't exactly look like a member of the peace and love set anymore.

But instead of Led Zeppelin's latest on the single dash speaker CHEF was running its hourly newscast. The Mark Simson story was there, complete with reference to Stubby Booker. So much for tuning in to tune it all out.

A set of headlights appeared in the distance behind me. They were approaching quickly, even though I was doing nearly 60 miles an hour. The closer the lights came, the more uneasy I felt, my paranoia overcoming common sense. In a matter of a few seconds the lights were within ten feet of my rear bumper. Then five feet, three feet, then they were so close I couldn't see them anymore. Couldn't see them, but knew exactly where they were.

I stepped on the gas, but still couldn't get the head lights to reappear. You can only go so fast with a Ford Falcon that has a six cylinder with a taste for oil. At 75 the steering wheel began to shake. I followed suit, my heart racing faster than the car.

Still the headlights remained hidden. The angry roar of a big block V-8 came from my trunk.

We roared through the village of Adamsville, which was illuminated only by a half dozen scattered streetlights. The sleepy silence of the town was utterly shattered by the sound of screaming engines and squealing tires as both our cars struggled to make the curve after the bridge.

By this point I was too scared to think. The flight response was at its height, telling me to get away, NOW. No tricks, no confrontation, just get to hell out of here. I could feel the sweat on my hands on the wheel as I began breathing hard through my mouth. I leaned forward, as if it helped me get further away from the roaring monster on my ass.

Then the headlights appeared in the mirror on my front fender. The headlights pulled up alongside and suddenly I was face to face with two men in a Plymouth Satellite. They had the radio cranked up and the windows down. The passenger wagged his tongue at me like a demon as they pulled ahead.

By this point we were coming into East Farnham. The Satellite, now well ahead of me, suddenly slammed on its brakes and slid out of control. It veered to the left, then the right. With a final screech of rubber on pavement it went off the road, skidding across a gravel parking lot and into a parked car.

At midnight Tuesday morning the bar, DuChene's, is almost always closed. The only car in the yard belonged to a regular named Dan, who was too drunk to drive home, so the barmaid left him to sleep it off inside. The crash didn't wake him up.

I pulled into the yard, my lights shining on the Satellite, which now looked somewhat like it was trying to mount the much smaller Datsun that brought it to a halt. The front wheels were off the ground, and the passenger door hung open. The only thing I could hear now was the blood pumping through my ears.

At first I didn't know what to do. Did these guys want to kill me? If I went to help, what would they do? I couldn't just leave them there, as much as I wanted to. After hesitating for a few seconds, I opted to go to a neighbour's house to call for help. The neighbour would at least then go with me to see if they survived.

I knocked at the door of this tiny little house and was met by an older gent in a housecoat. He'd already heard the crash, so he knew what was going on. When I told him about the chase he decided it was best to bring his shotgun along to check on the victims. He called the cops and we set off.

My first view of the accident didn't really show the extent of what happened. From the opposite side it was obvious just how fast these guys were going. The front of the Satellite had pushed right up into the back seat of the Datsun. Hot antifreeze from the larger car was now gushing into the interior of its victim, sending sweet smelling steam into the night air.

The front windshield bore two spider webs where the men's heads had hit hard. Both were unconscious and possibly dead, I couldn't tell. Their faces were covered in blood and sweat that pasted their hair to their heads. The driver, whose bare arm sported a Grateful Dead tattoo, was draped over the steering wheel. I didn't know what to do. The old man wasn't much help either. He nudged me forward. As I stepped ahead he raised his shotgun to his shoulder, at the ready.

Gingerly I approached the driver's side, with only the pale glow of a yard light to see by. I touched the man's arm, but there was no response. With a firmer grip I managed to pry him back from the steering wheel and into a normal sitting position, with his head tilted back. He swallowed then jerked, coughing and trying desperately to breathe. The body convulsed as the eyes opened in an expression of sheer terror. He looked at me, the eyes pleading, child-like.

"He's choking on something!" the old man chirped in. "I think he's got something stuck in his throat!"

I looked around, as if someone or something would appear to make it go away. Nothing did. It was up to me. The old man stood like a statue.

The convulsions got worse. My shirt was soaked in sweat by now, my heart pounding even faster than it had been during the car chase.

I reached in and gently grabbed the man's head, forcing his mouth open. Blood, not air came out, as his arms began flailing wildly, knocking the rear view mirror off the windshield. It became obvious I was going to have to fish out whatever was blocking his breathing.

Inserting my finger into the bleeding mouth I could feel bits of broken teeth and the warm wetness of saliva and blood. Then the tongue, and something else. I gently grabbed it between my finger and thumb as the man began a new round of convulsions, biting down on my fingers with broken teeth, splitting skin. I pulled it out and the man began breathing, gasping for air.

There, clutched between my two fingers was the stub of a cigar, rammed down his throat when he hit the windshield.

The ambulance pulled in as I stood there, examining the stump of cigar. I was calm now, the adrenaline having pushed me beyond the point of being scared. I dropped the cigar onto the gravel as the ambulance attendants pushed me aside to get at the two men in the Satellite. I hadn't even heard them arrive.

A couple of minutes later the cops arrived. Flashers were everywhere, casting hues of red and blue, and then yellow as the tow truck arrived. In the middle of it all Dan, the guy who owned the Datsun, woke up, still very drunk, and came out of the bar to see what happened. Unable to figure out the situation, he stumbled back into the bar. He'd have more than a hangover to deal with in the morning.

As I was explaining things to one of the cops my adrenaline rush started to subside. First I began to laugh uncontrollably, happy to be alive I guess. Then I got cold, becoming keenly aware that I was wearing a T-shirt soaked in sweat and blood in the middle of the night. That was followed by a new round of the sweats. Then I dropped to my knees and threw up.

The cop, who I expect had been through this kind of thing before, casually kicked some gravel over the puke with his shoe. He suggested they take me to the emergency room, to be sure I wasn't going into shock. At least that's what I think he said.

Ten minutes later I was at the Brome-Missisquoi Perkins Hospital in Cowansville, lying on a stretcher. Though I managed to avoid going into shock, I did spend the next hour fighting waves of panic, sweating and freezing. When it finally calmed down I asked if I could go home. The cop was still there, and he came over to talk to me again.

"Who in hell were those guys anyway?" I asked, getting back some of my composure.

"Fred Birches and Johnny Swett. Swett's wife showed up here a few minutes ago. She said the boys were out on a tear, been drinking since lunch time."

"Do they work for Stubby Booker?" I asked, though I felt a little silly as I did so. His eyebrows raised a little.

"These aren't exactly church going boys, but they aren't in Stubby's league. They just like to drink a little too much. Why?"

I gave him a quick rundown of the court story, and the evening's events.

He looked thoughtful for a few seconds, then broke into a grin.

"You writers sure have vivid imaginations," he said. "From where I sit, Stubby Booker likes the attention. He likes being able to rub it in our faces by getting his name in the paper and then walking away. Slippery little bastard."

The cop, who's name I don't think I ever heard, then said that Birches, the driver, had some broken ribs, a concussion and was going to need some dental surgery. Swett, the passenger, had a broken leg, a concussion of his own and a selection of broken ribs. Both would recover from their little bender, given some time. Dangerous driving and impaired driving charges were most likely headed their way. In 1975 that meant a fine and a few demerit points.

A few minutes later I checked out and the cop, now joined by his partner, gave me a lift back to the house in Brigham. By the time I showered and got into bed the clock was grinding towards 5 a.m. Jen was up too, and wanted an explanation. At least this time I had a good one.

***

Sleep that night was all too brief, and didn't come easily. It hardly came at all, and when it did, it failed to be restful.

In my dream I'm sitting in the passenger seat of an enormous Buick Roadmaster. Dad is driving, rolling a cigarette at the same time. I'm a child, as I always am in my dreams of him. Because I've missed him so I don't take notice of where we are, or know where we're going. It doesn't matter. I'm with my dad.

He steers with his elbows as he focuses his attention on the final tuck and roll, like a skilled craftsman. A skilled craftsman who is also driving a car.

"Got a taste of it, didn't you?"

"A taste of what?"

"What it's really like out here in the country."

"I've met a lot of people out here and they're nothing like that. Besides, these guys were just out drinking."

"Pretty hard, from the looks."

"People drink hard in the city too, dad."

"Ready to move that wife of yours someplace better?"

"I just got here. I haven't even been here long enough to get a job someplace else. Besides, where would I go?"

He says nothing, scratching a wooden match on the dash to light up. It may only be a dream, but I can smell the smoke as it comes out of his nose, hitting the steering wheel before dissolving into the air. It's the way he always smells. He seems to be considering what he's going to say next, staring at the tip of the cigarette clenched between the battered knuckles of his left hand, which sits perched on the top of the steering wheel.

But that thought is cut off as his eyes open wider and he reefs on the steering wheel, throwing the car into a skid. I hear the sound of rattling gravel and see him leaning into the turn. My head hits the dash, making an explosion in my head and I'm awake.

Back in my house in Brigham, where all is quiet and dark. My heart is pounding, and even though the dream is over I'm scrambling to figure out what I'm going to tell him next. I can hear the slow mechanical grind of the alarm clock as it labours through the night. A streetlight reflects off the far wall.

My bedroom is filled with the lingering smell of cigarettes.

8

Every morning Stubby Booker had breakfast at John's Cantine, on the Adamsville Road just outside of Granby. It was really more like a small restaurant, frequented by a selection of locals who probably should have been working. Everybody knew everybody else, and gossip was as much a part of the breakfast as the eggs, bacon and the thick black coffee.

Wednesday morning the talk was all about the Granby Leader-Mail story about the cow thief. What in hell was Stubby doing getting his fingers into stealing beef? Didn't he have enough to do? Is there anything that this man isn't into?

One man, an older farmer, put forward the idea that this Simson character blurted it out to get a lighter sentence. Booker may be a lot of things, but he's no cow thief, he said. Kid just wanted to get off, figured if he led the cops to a bigger fish they'd let him go.

The others at the counter immediately shouted him down. You can't put anything past Booker, they said. He'd probably rape little old ladies if he could make a buck at it.

The conversation came to an abrupt halt when the shiny GMC pickup pulled into the yard. When Stubby walked in he knew by the silence something was going on. It pissed him off that these people, who he visited with every morning, had been talking about him. He hadn't heard anything, but he knew it was true. Probably something to do with that story he heard on the radio about Mark Simson.

As he walked by one of the tables he grabbed a Leader-Mail from the hands of one of the old men having breakfast. The atmosphere of contempt for this mean little man was long gone, replaced with a quiet reverence. Reverence inspired by fear.

By the time he was at his usual seat at the counter Grace, the waitress, had already poured his coffee.

"Good morning sir," she said before beating a hasty retreat to kitchen, as if there was something there she forgot to do.

His first glimpse at the headline confirmed that he had indeed been the talk of the place: "Simson says Stubby made him do it."

Booker was known as a man with a hot temper. But he was smarter than that, knowing that there were times when fits of rage could serve a purpose, and times when they could land you in jail. Everything Stubby Booker did served a purpose.

He glanced at the byline: Dave Rogers. That little prick. "Where the fuck did he get off even mentioning my name?" he thought.

Everyone in John's Cantine watched to see what Stubby's reaction would be. His face turned red for an instant, the blood pressure rising beneath his pale skin. His body shook for a second, like he was about to explode. His knuckles cracked under the force of clenching fists.

Then he broke out laughing.

"That little prick Simson said he worked for me?" he roared. "That's me, big time cow thief. Better hang on to your cows folks, 'cause I'm gonna steal them all. Maybe I'll steal your dog while I'm at it."

Tears began rolling down his face, all traces of rage gone, replaced by hilarity.

"Who would be stupid enough to think I'd steal cows, let alone hire a moron like Mark Simson to do it for me?" he said, the challenging tone in his voice unmistakable. "I've got a legitimate business, and that little prick wants to drag me into his two bit cow stealing operation."

Booker knew that it was the question they were all asking, even though none of them dared ask. He decided to give them a bit of a show.

"Well this'll give the cops something to chew on for awhile, won't it? Those pricks always think I'm up to something, but they can't pull their heads out of their asses long enough to do anything intelligent. If they knew their asses from their elbows they'd leave me alone and get on with their jobs."

"What do you think this kid was doing with the cows?" asked a thin old man in the corner. "Not exactly easy to get rid of, like a TV set."

"How the fuck should I know?" came the reply. "This little shithead wanted to give the cops something to get them off his ass, so he gives up my name, 'cause he knows they're pissed at me from that time last year when they raided my place and didn't find nothing."

That raid had indeed been the talk of the region, and front page news in the Granby Liar. The police came up with nothing stolen, nothing illegal. Stubby walked away, as angry and defiant as ever. The cops were left to lick their wounds once again.

By the time Stubby's bacon and eggs arrived the conversation had moved on to other topics. His voice returned to its usual smouldering angry tone, and the room broke up into a half dozen quiet conversations about sex, the weather, taxes, politics and sex. The usual.

After settling up the bill, Stubby stuck his head into the kitchen to speak to John, who was taking a case of ground beef out of the freezer to thaw.

"How's that new meat supplier of yours?" Stubby asked.

"He's fine," smiled John. "Get's me good quality meat and charges a hell of a lot less than Blackstone did. No complaints."

Stubby climbed into the GMC, the copy of the paper under his arm. He pulled away, heading towards Cowansville, driving at a sedate pace. Though it wasn't particularly hot, a thin film of sweat was forming above his thick dark eyebrow.

Three miles later Stubby pulled onto a side road, drove for another mile and then came to a halt, switching off the engine.

Then he let his temper off the leash.

For the next several minutes Stubby Booker cursed, screamed and pounded on the dash of his truck. He didn't like Rogers before, and he damn well hated him now. That little prick was trouble. Came from trouble.

He then whipped the Granby Liar out of the window. As it hit the ground he pulled out a long barreled .38 revolver from under the seat. Each time he fired the paper danced and shredded. The kick and sound of each shot was a release of his own tension.

Before the sound of the shots finished echoing off of the surrounding hillsides, Stubby started the truck up again and drove away. Time to get on with the day's business.

Simson's time in jail, in this world for that matter, would be short. As for Rogers, Stubby wasn't sure what he was going to do just yet.

9

What sleep I did get that morning was fitful, full of images of possessed men in big cars chasing me to God knows where. A few times I woke, surges of fear coursing through my body. It wasn't a very hot day, but I had the sweats.

By 11 a.m. it was obvious that sleep was out of the question. But work was out of the question too, so I called in sick. I gave the details to John McAuslan, who planned on doing the story. It took a little convincing, but I got him to agree to leave my name out of it. It was hardly my shining moment in the sun.

As I sat on the porch King wandered up to say hello, almost as if he sensed my frame of mind. He looked at me thoughtfully before depositing his head on my lap.

King had taken well to country living, wandering off whenever he could to explore the nearby fields. Unfortunately he was also quick to pick up that country dog habit of rolling in something dead. The smell overpowered any feelings of deep affection I had at the moment, and I hauled him off to be tied up in the back yard.

"He's just telling you he loves you," quipped Jen. She was on her day off, and had taken to her role as my nurse for the day, checking on me regularly to see if I was okay.

"Not exactly the kind of love I was looking for," I replied, reaching for her behind as she walked by.

It was noon by then, and having a beer seemed like the thing to do. We had one left in the house and payday was still two days off. Jen decided to let me have the whole thing, pouring herself an iced tea.

Brigham was unusually quiet, with almost no traffic. In the distance I could hear the rhythmic clacking of a bailer. The second cut, so I'd been told. The store could have been closed, except that the door hung open. The lights were off inside, and no motion could be seen from where we sat on our porch. I sat and watched dust devils twist their way down the street, venturing a few dozen feet before vanishing into the nothingness from which they had come.

By lunch time the after effects of the car chase had pretty much worn off, and I began to feel a little more lively. I wasn't used to stress of that kind, and my body didn't know how to handle it, or the hangover that followed. It's never easy to come off of a high level adrenaline rush, but the only other alternative is to stay panicked all of the time. That's really not my style.

The only minor rush I got was when I went over to the store to see how the paper looked. I glanced at the story about Simson, and wondered what Booker thought.

For a few moments I felt a twinge of guilt. I had written a story that dragged a man into a crime for which there was no evidence that he was involved. But then again I was just reporting what was said in court, and the judge hadn't tried to stop me. Besides, judging from everything else I'd heard about Booker at the Barrel last night, it wasn't as if I was pointing the finger at the little old lady next door.

By the time I'd left the store life was pretty much back to normal. For what seemed like the first time I took notice of the majestic maples that lined the street. Spectacular pillars thrusting thousands of green-gloved fingers to the skies. They had been there long before I arrived, and chances are they would still be there long after I was gone, providing shade and comfort for generations to come.

Later in the day I got a ride from Steve Farnham to pick up my car, which was still sitting in the yard of DuChene's. It didn't seem to be any worse for wear after the high-speed chase, in fact it seemed to run a little smoother. I was glad for that, because I simply couldn't afford another car. No car meant no job, and I really didn't want my career to come to a halt when it had barely begun.

That evening was spent quietly at home with Jen, doing a lot of talking and catching up on how we were both doing. Jen's life was getting busier all the time, and her adjustment to life in the boonies seemed to be coming along well. I was still working more than the 40 hours a week I was paid for, but I had calmed down somewhat on the workaholic thing.

We talked a bit about the things we missed in the city, like the great restaurants, close friends and the nightlife. Though we'd only been away from Montreal for a couple of months, life there was quickly fading to memories.

We also talked about us, and how we were doing and where we wanted to be going. It was a frank discussion, with subjects that required a negotiated settlement. There were no angry words like there had been in the past when these subjects came up, and in the end we agreed on almost everything.

And this time there was love making at the end of it.

The next day I was back at work, back at the job of going into a situation blind, and coming out of it having to know enough to make it sound like I was an authority on the subject. That was the challenge, and it was also the rush. A rush that was quickly becoming addictive.

Upon my arrival at the office my coworkers presented me with an old trophy that someone had won God knows when. It had been cleaned up and a Hot Wheels Ford Falcon glued to the top. Over the name plate was glued a sign that read "Dave Rogers, winner of the 1975 Drunk Driving Demolition Derby."

The trophy was followed by the presentation of a new set of seat covers, under the assumption that the old ones had been soiled during my little high speed adventure.

"By the way, when you're out there playing Jackie Stewart on the roads and you finally get yourself killed, which one of us gets to write the deado?" asked John McAuslan.

"Try drawing straws," I replied.

That's what a serious accident came down to for a reporter. Doing a deado. It was just another way of putting a comfortable cushion between yourself and the person you were writing about who was now dead. To an outsider it might sound a little callous, and it is. But if you worry about these things too much you can't do your job. You can't do your job if all you can see in your head is someone with a face and a mother and a father slowly hemorrhaging to death in a car while firefighters try desperately to drag them out.

To be fair, reporters treat each other as bad or worse than the general public. Before I was on the scene a Granby Liar reporter qualified for an exchange program that saw him sent to be a war correspondent in Vietnam for a few months. The office immediately set up a betting pool on which part of him would get shot off first. No one even thought of betting he'd come home with a dose of clap.

My first story back had to do with a prison break at the federal penitentiary in Cowansville. Two guys managed to sneak out in a laundry truck, like something out of the movies. They then stole a car from a nearby home, drove for a couple of miles and then ditched it. Then they went on and stole another car. They were headed for Montreal and the anonymity of the big city, but were caught at 6 a.m. by a provincial police roadblock.

It had all the elements of a fun story to write, a good one to get me back into the swing of things.

The visual aspect of the story pretty much over with, I called Fernand Dubois for the details. He'd heard about my little adventure from his buddies, and decided to give me a little teasing as well.

"You know speeding is a serious infraction of the highway safety code," he said. "You're supposed to leave that kind of thing to those of us who can handle high speed responsibly."

"So you mean cops can handle being chased by drunken goons better than me?" I shot back.

"We have guns. It adds to the sport of it all."

From there the conversation turned back to the prison escape. The two inmates were wired on some sort of homemade booze prisoners brew up behind the walls. It was poorly planned, but they got lucky. Until they hit the roadblock. Now the two men, who had been in the process of serving three and five year terms, were facing new charges stemming from the escape. Chances of parole also went out the window, and Dubois said they would most likely be split up and sent to other institutions.

"If you want anything more about these guys you'll have to call the prison and ask for a guy named Hayes," Dubois said.

I was putting the finishing touches on my notes and getting ready to hang up on Dubois. This is usually the point where you're trying to carry a conversation while wracking your brain to see if anything had been missed.

"So what was this that you thought those guys had something to do with Stubby Booker?" Dubois asked.

"How did you know about that?" I replied, feeling a little startled. How in hell did he know about that? I guessed he had talked to the cop on duty, and it came up.

"Well you can relax. I heard Stubby had a good laugh over the whole thing. That little bastard loves to get his name in the paper, especially when he's getting away with something."

"How did you hear that he's laughing about it?" I sensed that he knew more than he was letting on, and that he was enjoying it. I also sensed he wasn't going to give me the whole story.

"Word gets around in small towns," came the cryptic response.

Knowing that he was going to string me along I decided it was time to cut things off. I told him I didn't particularly care what Booker thought, and said good-bye.

I pulled a 12 inch story out of the prison break, accompanied by a rather generic-looking pic taken at the prison gates by one of our free-lance photographers. From there I moved on to a bit about swimmers in Granby's Lake Boivin getting a rash from some parasite that lived in duck shit. That was followed the next day by a bit on a new zoning bylaw, and another story on a series of break-ins in East Farnham.

In newspapers you never sit still for very long. That suited me just fine.

10

For the next couple of weeks, things rolled along nicely. There was plenty of news, though none of it particularly controversial. In other words, there was plenty to write, but not a lot of excitement.

But this quiet time did give me a chance to settle in a little more in my new surroundings. I'd been in the Townships for a couple of months now, but had been too busy to take much notice of anything around me that wasn't the subject of a story. Other than my co-workers I still had no friends, having barely even spoken to the neighbours.

The Townships is a rural region that has just about every kind of terrain going. Steep, hunchbacked mountains, rolling hills and open prairies where families operated huge farms were all there. A mix of maples and huge fir trees sprouted here and there, usually surrounded by smaller stands of birch, cedar and poplar.

At one time virgin stands of gigantic timber blanketed the region, but almost all of them had been felled by pioneers and lumberjacks. In 1975 almost every home in the region had a Vilas table, made when the furniture plant sought out every maple tree it could find within forty miles of the Cowansville plant just after World War Two.

The scars of those assaults on the land had faded over the years, replaced by a new brand of spectacular beauty. In our first few weeks living here we fled to Montreal at the end of the week to surround ourselves with the comforts of friends and familiar old haunts. But now, with the end of summer almost upon us, we spent a couple of weekends exploring our new surroundings.

The change in Jen was amazing. The frustration and isolation of the first weeks in Brigham quickly gave way, and I slowly began to realize that she knew more people around here than I did. The Weaver's Guild was the beginning of it all, bringing her out of her shell. She was no longer the woman who followed her husband out from the city, evolving instead into a member of the community.

I, on the other hand, was having a harder time of it. I found the people somewhat standoffish, especially when they found out I worked for the paper. A bad reputation is hard to get rid of, and I was brought into the equation under the dark cloud of the Granby Liar. People liked reading the paper, it seemed, but they didn't want their names in it.

During our explorations we also did a little digging into my own past, visiting Dunham, a little town south of Cowansville. The tombstones of three generations of my family were there, including my father's.

The first ancestor to arrive was Sheltus Rogers, an American who decided at the age of 60 that he wasn't going to be in the States to see the turn of the century. He came to Dunham and was one of the early people to start an apple orchard in the region. By the time he died at 74 years old, the orchard was on its way to being a success.

Then came grandpa, a man I met only as a very young child. Jake and his four brothers made the orchard thrive, and then saw other possibilities with the arrival of prohibition in the 1930's. The Rogers family got into the apple cider business, with most of the product hauled through the woods to Vermont.

Apple Jack was particularly popular with Jake's southern customers. Not wanting to be bothered with a still, Apple Jack was made by freezing cider outside in the winter or in the ice house the rest of the time. The alcohol and the sweetest parts of the cider wouldn't freeze, offering a sugary, high octane drink.

Jake was never caught in the smuggling game, though his brothers did have their share of run-ins with the law. One brother, Francis, developed a drinking problem and died in the late 1940's. The other two brothers took their earnings from the smuggling operation and headed out west following the end of Prohibition.

Jake stayed on the farm, marrying a girl from Richford, Vermont. They had two kids, Dave Sr. and Phyllis. Aunt Phyllis died early in 1974 in a shotgun shack of a house across the valley from the family farm. We rarely visited over the years, and the family bond had been practically non-existent. Limited mostly to Christmas cards and rare phone calls.

When I was born in 1946 we were living in the same house my great grandfather built. Grandpa was living in a nursing home, his mind destroyed by "old timer's disease," the locals called it. Grandma lived with us, a fact I'm sure made life hell for my mom, who moved in when she married dad.

Right around the time I turned five my dad announced one day that we were moving. Within a few short weeks we were living in Montreal, in a cramped little apartment in the NDG district. My dad got a job working in construction, climbing in the high steel downtown.

The day after I turned 9, my father's luck with heights ran out.

I always remembered that my dad showed no interest in coming back to the country. At the time I figured he hated living in the sticks. But when he died his will said he wanted to be buried behind the Anglican church in Dunham. I guess he wanted to come home after all.

Nineteen years later I was sitting in the Falcon with Jen looking at a farm where I was born that had been in my family for three generations. But now I was an outsider, with no right to tread on the land that was once so much a part of my family. The memories were vague, and the landmarks altered enough by time to draw attention to the fact that I didn't belong. The No Trespassing sign on the fencepost at the end of the driveway said it all.

We spent the Saturday afternoon of Labour Day weekend cruising the Dunham hills, while I told Jen stories about my ancestors. She'd heard them before, but was patient enough to quietly listen to them once again. We paid a brief visit to the family plot in the Dunham graveyard before heading back home.

In a spirit of exploration we decided to take the back roads to Brigham, eventually finding ourselves on a road called the Tenth Range. It was straight as a pin and rough as hell, forcing us to slow down to a crawl. The Falcon shook and rattled, the rusted front fenders flapping in the cross wind. But the new seat covers were plush and comfy.

In the distance I could see a pickup truck pulled over, with three men standing in the ditch. There was some frantic activity going on, as the men heaved black garbage bags into the truck. Their work stopped suddenly when we were about a hundred yards away, and one of the men looked at me with a distinct hint of fear in his eyes.

As we passed the cross wind brought into the car the smell of freshly harvested pot.

"Tis the season," Jen said.

"Do you think they could be a little more obvious?" I replied. "They might as well paint 'We're Harvesting Weed' on the side of the truck."

That night we treated ourselves to supper at the Roma Pizzeria in Cowansville, followed by High Plains Drifter on channel 12.

Though Sunday was supposed to be a day off, the reporters were asked to turn out for the Big Brome Fair. Brome is a tiny village east of

Cowansville, comprised of barely three hundred souls. But every Labor Day it plays host to the largest agricultural fair in the region, attracting tens of thousands of people.

In an effort to attract readers the Granby Leader-Mail faithfully set up a tent there every year, with reporters and volunteers selling subscriptions and chatting up the readership.

It was a bright day with just a hint of the crisp fall weather to come. Our tent was set up outside the Main Building, and the smell of cooking food from Derby's Cantine was carried into our little canvas dome by the late summer breeze. Around us milled people of all shapes and sizes.

Here and there couples could be spotted, decked out in matching T-shirt and jeans. Women staggered by on high heels unsuited to the soft earth of the fairgrounds. A Foghat tune could be heard in the distance, coming from one of the rides.

Most of the visitors to the tent were older, stopping in to renew subscriptions they'd held for decades. They were the first to complain if we missed something or if they didn't get their news on a given day, but they were also the first to put their money where their mouth is and buy the paper.

"And which one are you?" came the inevitable enquiry.

"I'm Dave Rogers, sir."

"I've got a neighbour you should do a story on. That rotten bugger's cows get out all of the time and shit all over my lawn. You wouldn't believe it, but the other day when I called him to come get the bastards, he shows up with a hunting knife and threatens me..."

From these little conversations I gleaned story ideas about the local women's guild, an old lady that was turning 100, and an old man who liked to get drunk and relive World War Two on his farm, complete with an old Lee Enfield assault rifle and live ammunition.

"My God! You must be young David Rogers!" came the comment from a heavy set old lady renewing her subscription. She had a nervous habit of opening and closing her mouth even when she wasn't speaking, and her tongue would dart out like a snake's, keeping the lips perpetually moist.

"That's me."

"I'd recognize those eyes anywhere. You're the spitting image of your father."

"You knew my dad?"

"Oh my yes. He was quite the man in his day. Almost notorious you might say."

"Where did you know him from?" I asked, my curiosity piqued.

"I grew up down the hill from the Rogers farm. Of course you wouldn't remember me from when you lived there. You were just a youngster."

"Oh, wow," I said. "I haven't met anybody around here yet who knew my family. But it's not like I've had a lot of time to socialize, other than for work."

As I spoke her mouth remained in perpetual motion, the tongue darting continually. I found it an effort not to start doing the same thing myself.

"In your grandfather's day I used to work at the farm, cleaning house for a time when your grandmother was sick. That was before your mom came into the picture and took over things."

"After your mom and dad left for the city I helped Diane out again, but she was too far gone and died about six months later."

"You know I don't even really remember her," I said, feeling somewhat ashamed that my memory didn't contain much more than fragments from before the age of five.

"I always wondered where you people went in such a hurry. It's really too bad your father didn't come out for the funeral. It was his mother after all."

Her words jarred a vague memory in me. I remembered scraps of that funeral, of faces I'd never seen before or since. I remembered mom and aunt Phyllis, dressed in black on a cold fall afternoon, crying. My dad wasn't in those memories, though I'd always figured he must have been there.

I was still letting this newfound information about my father sink in when out of the corner of my eye I noticed a big boned woman talking to a large stocky man with a thick beard about 20 feet away. He pointed towards me and she immediately began walking my way, with a purpose.

Ten feet away she scooped up a pottery jug from a display table. Then I heard an explosion in my head and everything went black for a second.

I still haven't been able to figure out just how the next 30 seconds of my life went. I remember lying on the ground clutching the side of my head. I remember the enraged woman standing over me, screaming, but I heard nothing.

Instinctively I kicked at her, but missed. Scrambling to my feet, I was trying desperately to figure out what was going on. Then I saw the pottery jug again, swinging my way. I ducked, and it whistled over my head. It came back quickly, catching me in the ribs. The air went out of my lungs and wouldn't go back in. I was on my knees again.

The next thing I remember I had pinned the woman on the Granby Leader-Mail table, one hand on her throat and the other on her right arm, which was still holding the pottery jug. I was shaking, she was crying.

The large man pushed me aside and took hold of the woman.

"Mrs. Simson, calm down, it's not his fault," he said.

She let out a squeal of anguish through the tears. Unable to complete her attack, she went limp, sobbing uncontrollably. He continued speaking to her softly. I couldn't hear anything except the ringing in my ears.

"What the hell is going on here?" said Harry Bankroft, who appeared out of nowhere. I didn't even know he was pulling fair duty. He handed me a handkerchief. "You're bleeding."

By now a sizable crowd had gathered, drawn by the commotion. The woman was still being held by the large man when she made a final, but ineffective lunge at me.

"You bastard, you killed my boy!"

11

I was still feeling rather dazed when Bankroft grabbed me by the arm and dragged me off through the crowd. Despite the cool breeze I was sweating as he dragged me into the men's washroom.

"Jesus H. Christ. What the hell have you gone and done to yourself now?" Bankroft said. "This isn't exactly the place to be getting into a scrap."

"I don't know what happened. One second I was talking to this nice old lady and then all hell breaks loose."

Bankroft had wet down a paper towel and was trying to dab it at the gash opened up on the upper part of my cheek, just in front of my ear. His attempts at administering first aid were rough, clumsy.

"You're a really crappy nurse," I said, wincing as he dabbed at the cut again.

"Well you're a really crappy prize fighter," came the reply, followed by another shot with the paper towel.

A few minutes later Steve Farnham appeared at the door.

"She's gone guys. That was Lillian Simson, the mom of your cow thief. Apparently he killed himself in the Cowansville pen."

Bankroft and I just looked at each other. Pieces began clicking into place.

"She thinks my story on him had something to do with it?"

"She was still babbling on about it when that big mountain of a guy took her away. Kept saying your story put him on Stubby Booker's shit list. Said he'd still be alive if you hadn't said what you did."

The information was there, but the meaning of it wasn't sinking in. I didn't know what to think, how to feel. Men filed back and forth, making use of the stainless steel trough that served as a urinal at the fairgrounds.

"That's bullshit," came Bankroft's sudden reply. He said no more for a moment.

"Steve, get over to the P.A. booth and page his wife," he said, speaking as if I wasn't even there. "She'd better take him home and get him cleaned up."

Farnham left without a word, man on a mission.

"As for you, get your sorry ass out of here and get cleaned up. Tomorrow's a holiday, so take it easy. Tuesday morning I want you to get going on this first thing and find out what's happening."

"Is this really a good idea?" I asked. "Aren't I already a little too close to this one?"

"That's bullshit. You were doing your job, nothing more, nothing less. It's not up to you if some kid off's himself. You know the case, so either keep doing your job or start looking for a new one."

Looking back on it I think that was the best Harry Bankroft could do at being sympathetic. He lived in a hard world filled with hard rules.

We stepped out of the washroom just as I saw Jen frantically pushing her way through the crowd, with Farnham lagging behind. She wrapped her arms around me, painfully reminding me that I had also taken a shot to the ribs with that damned jug.

That night Jen was in full nurse mode, tending my wounds and making me comfortable on the couch. Hot tea and bag of ice was her answer to my problems, though I would have preferred a shot of morphine to go with it.

"You're staying here tonight, so I won't be running into your bruises in the dark," she said. "Our bed wouldn't do you any favors anyways, with the springs poking up through everywhere."

I came out of my little altercation with Mrs. Simson with a half-inch gash on my cheek between my right eye and ear. The side of my face had swollen, and the blow had popped a vessel in my eye, filling it with blood. My ear grew along with the side of my face, and the whole region was painful to the slightest touch.

Along with that the ribs on the right side of my spine were now home to a bruise about six inches long and three inches wide. It hurt to breathe, and I couldn't lay on my back or on my right side.

Psychologically I wasn't much better. Bankroft said I was doing my job, and he was right. Still I couldn't help feeling waves of guilt at the thought that what I had written could have driven a young man to kill himself.

My thoughts were also mixed with feelings of paranoia. Would there be other angry relatives out there? Would they come after me? If I did the follow up story on Mark Simson's suicide, would they think of it as yet another provocation?

The pain managed to interfere with my darkest thoughts, pushing them away to a safe distance. I lay on the couch on my left side and stared at the black and white Zenith. Shows came and went until I drifted off to sleep.

King, perhaps feeling cheated at not having his usual night time use of the couch, dropped to the floor next to me, letting out a deep sigh as he went to sleep.

I emerged from the dark silence of sleep into a vision of the family farm. But the house looks run down, uncared for, the cracks in some of the windows, panes missing from others. The wind is blowing hard, pulling at my coat in a vain attempt to draw me away. The clouds above are roiling by in a ragged race, too busy to rain.

I walk around the back of the house, and there's a wing that is totally abandoned. Though this doesn't exist in reality, I know it, and know that my family has blocked off the doors, leaving it to its own fate as they struggle to live out their lives in the main building. They are smaller people as a result, turning inwards on themselves as they seek to leave their burdens in the wing, to crumble into oblivion and maybe, just maybe, they will go away.

In their haste to close it off the family has left something behind. Though I don't know what it is, I know it is in the abandoned rooms. The floors are unsafe, and I have to keep to the sides of the room, avoid the open areas. Rain has been leaking in through the ceiling, slicking the sloped floors. Search as I might, I found nothing.

When I awoke the house was dark, the TV silent. I couldn't ever remember feeling so lonely.

Early Monday morning I decided I was going to have to see a doctor to get something for the pain. He told me I probably should have gotten stitches for the cut, but it was too late now. X-rays showed my ribs were all intact. I got a prescription for codeine, a fresh bandage for the cut, and a warning to take it easy for a few days.

Tuesday morning I went back to work.

I got to work a little later than usual, walking in just after 11 a.m. After procrastinating for about a half hour I made my first call to John Hayes, the assistant warden at the Cowansville penitentiary who usually handled the press. Despite the English name he spoke with a faint French accent. He would say "dat" instead of "that."

"So I understand that an inmate named Mark Simson committed suicide sometime in the last couple of days," I began the interview.

"An inmate was found dead Friday night," Hayes said. "We have not released his name for de time being."

"Am I right in saying that it was Simson?"

"Where did you get dat information, sir?"

"I ran into his mother the other day."

A moment of silence.

"Off de record, yes. On the record I am not allowed to release dat information."

"Can you tell me what happened?"

"On Friday night during the head count before lights out we came up one short. A search was conducted and Simson was found about an hour later in one of de woodworking shops. He was hanging from one of de heating pipes."

"Did he commit suicide?" I asked, the vision of the cow thief who smelled like manure appeared in my head, swinging slightly.

"I can't really say much more except dat it is being treated as a suspicious death. The investigation has been turned over to the Quebec Police Force."

"When you say it is a suspicious death, do you mean he may have been murdered?"

"I did not say dat sir. All I said was he did not die of natural causes, so an investigation is necessary to confirm what happened."

"So what happens next?"

"You'll have to call Fernand Dubois about that. The investigators were in over the weekend, so he may have something for you. The body has been removed from the establishment, probably for an autopsy."

I sensed there was something more to the situation than he let on, but I knew he wasn't going to let me get anywhere. I considered asking him again, and decided to give it one more shot.

"Is there reason to believe Simson was murdered?"

"You'll have to ask the provincials about dat, sir," came the curt reply.

Next up was Fernand Dubois. Having already done a dozen or so stories in which he acted as the official spokesman, he had become quite chummy.

"So you're calling about your friend, Mr. Simson?" he asked as soon as he heard my voice. "Heard you met up with his mother."

Does this guy hear about everything?

"Your little newspaper booth was just down from our big cop booth," he said. "By the time one of our boys went over to see what the fuss was about you were already gone. We didn't expect you'd be pressing charges."

While I wanted to like this guy, I found he was getting under my skin more and more. But I had a job to do, and was probably going to have to deal with Dubois at least until I got a better job at a bigger paper.

The first part of the interview went essentially the same as it had with Hayes. I didn't let on I knew the basics already, on the chance something new would pop up. It didn't.

"So what happens next with the investigation?" I asked.

"Simson's body has been sent out for an autopsy to confirm the cause of death. The coroner was off for the weekend, so we are waiting for the official results later today or early tomorrow. It could be interesting."

I could almost feel him wincing on the other end of the line. That last bit wasn't supposed to be said. But Dubois had a hard time stopping himself when he had something juicy. We had already joked about it in the newsroom.

"What do you mean by interesting?"

"I, er, mean it should confirm that he committed suicide."

"Come on Fernand," I said, trying to play the friendly card he began our little game with. "That doesn't sound interesting at all. Cough it up."

"Can we go off the record?"

Pens down everyone. "Okay."

"It looks like a suicide. However there are a couple of things that seem a little unusual. Simson looked like he'd been pretty badly beaten up. There were also marks on his wrists that looked like his hands had been tied."

Bingo.

"So it was a murder."

"Look, this can't get out until the autopsy is complete. When it is, I'll make a point of calling you first. But in the meantime you're going to have to sit on it."

You always hear the stories about the reporters who get information and then burn the guy they got it from. But if you do that in a small town pretty soon there's no one left to talk to. Dubois knew that if I burned him for the sake of a scoop he'd shut down on me. I wouldn't even be able to get a decent accident story out of him, or from the guy who replaced him once the shit stopped hitting the fan at HQ.

So I agreed to wait, but made it clear that the paper was going out tonight, and it would be old news for the Friday edition. There aren't very many opportunities for scoops when you work at a biweekly.

From there Dubois and I moved on to the typical cop check stuff, with him giving me a rundown on the events of the long weekend. Two accidents, one fatality. A break and enter at a home in Cowansville, with little information to go on. Otherwise it had been a quiet holiday weekend.

I spent the rest of the day writing up the results of the cop check and digging into a small stack of press releases that had been lying on the corner of my desk. The deado was turned into a story, while the rest were written up as news briefs.

At 4:45 I began to suspect that Dubois wasn't going to be calling me. I called him instead to make sure he didn't screw off and leave me without my story.

"He was murdered. The coroner confirmed that he died as a result of the hanging. He was apparently beaten and there was even a minor stab wound we missed. At some point before he died his hands and feet were tied. There were also indications that he may have been gagged as well."

"How in hell does that happen in a federal prison?" I asked.

"That's what we're going to have to figure out. Unfortunately it can be difficult to find who's responsible. Convicts don't like talking to the cops very much."

"But how can they get away with it? Aren't there supposed to be guards? Security?"

"We'll have to wait and see what the investigation shows. It was a long weekend and the staff levels were lower than usual, but that's not supposed to affect anything. Don't quote me on that last part."

I wrote up the story, starting with the details of the investigation. Then I moved on to Simson's past, giving a quick rundown of his previous offences and his most recent conviction for cattle rustling. I considered using the "Stubby Booker made me do it!" quote, but thought the better of it.

Bankroft was back to his usual sunny manner, taking my copy and grunting through a cloud of cigarette smoke. He had almost finished the first pack of the night, and number two was lying next to it, foil removed.

By 6:15 I was headed for home. My cheek had begun to throb and my bruised ribs were sore from leaning on a hard backed wooden chair all day. All I wanted at that moment was a cup of Jen's tea to wash down the codeine.

The image of the tortured and murdered Mark Simson came home with me.

12

The breakfast crowd at John's Cantine was hopping Tuesday morning with the latest story in the Granby Leader-Mail. Simson had been murdered and the story in the paper recalled the "Stubby Booker made me do it" quote. It didn't come out and accuse Stubby of ordering the little punk's death, but it might as well have.

"I told you that kid Simson was working for him!" the thin old man in the corner said. The comment had been generally agreed upon when he said it the first time, though the old man liked to think he was the one in the know.

John was keeping himself busy in the back. He didn't like the talk going around, knowing full well that his meat supplier was one of Stubby's associates. He bit his lip and made a point of paying close attention to the grill.

"How can he just go and order somebody killed?" asked a young lumberjack who smelled faintly of oil.

"Hell Stubby can pretty much do whatever Stubby wants," replied another.

"Hell, that kid probably pissed off the wrong guys in jail. Stubby probably ain't got nothin' to do wit' it," chirped in another. That comment was met with jeers from the others.

Once again the room fell silent as the shiny GMC pulled into the yard. The lumberjack and another man tried to strike up a conversation between themselves about the Montreal Canadiens. But the words were halting, distracted. Everyone else in the dirty little restaurant remained silent.

Stubby walked in, grabbing the Leader-Mail off of the counter and climbing onto a stool. The headline "Mark Simson murdered in Cowansville Pen" jumped off of the page.

"Little cow thief bought it," Stubby said quietly. He knew by the silence that it had been discussed already. He also had a hunch that something in the story was keeping these guys quieter than usual.

There, buried in the second half of the story: "Following his sentencing last month, Simson told the court that he had been forced to commit the crime by Roxton businessman Stubby Booker."

"What the fuck?" he said, caught off guard by the statement. He tensed, read the paragraph again. Nothing more was mentioned, just that one sentence, stuck in there in a way that changed everything.

Booker's neck began to change colours as he fought for control. That little bastard Rogers. Who in hell did he think he was? What was he trying to do? The veins began to bulge, as everyone waited for the explosion of rage.

He found his control, fighting back the urge to tell everyone how he wanted Rogers dead. Booker's life was about control, and everything was done to serve a purpose. He reminded himself of that.

"I'm going to sue that little cock sucker!" he roared loud enough to make the skinny old man jump in his seat. "How dare he drag me into this bullshit! Someone goes and off's the little bastard in prison and he thinks I'm in on it?"

"I don't think it's as bad as that," John said from behind the grill, which he was still staring at.

"First that little shit Simson goes and mentions my name and then he gets himself killed. Now this bastard at the Granby Liar goes and drags that up again, as if the cops don't have enough to chew on already. Do you know what it's like to run a goddam business with the cops snooping through your shit all of the time?"

"Last year when they raided my place I was with a customer. Turns out he had an outstanding warrant for some unpaid traffic tickets. They haul him away and he hasn't wanted to do business with me since. Bastard owes me money too!"

"Now to top it all off this shithead of a reporter goes and accuses me of having Simson killed. Well he's not going to get away with it! I'm a legitimate businessman and I have a reputation to protect. I'm going to sue his sorry ass! He'll regret ever having mentioned my name!"

* * *

Tuesday morning I slept late, having spent most of the night trying desperately to get comfortable. Jen made me take an extra codeine at about 4 a.m., and from then on I pretty much slept like a baby.

At 10 a.m. I was awake, and it was clear the codeine was beginning to wear off. I was still rubbing my eyes when I remembered that I had about 30 minutes to get to Granby for a press conference. Considering that Granby was nearly a half hour drive, my day was going to have to start in high gear.

Ten minutes later I rushed out the door. Jen had gone to work a couple of hours earlier. No time to make a lunch, no time to shower. I boiled some instant coffee while I got dressed. The Falcon started after about 30 seconds of cranking and several shots with the gas pedal, and I was gone.

I headed up des Érables at about 60 miles an hour, with the cup of coffee in an open mug perched between my legs. It was too hot to drink and the road was too rough to leave a full cup sitting there. I poured some of it out of the window as I crested the big hill. A dump truck coming the other way nearly took my arm off as I convulsively yanked the car back into my lane with my free hand.

Press conferences often start late. This morning I was going to have to count on that.

I pulled into the yard of the Simons plant, once known as Simons Saws. As the name would suggest they forged saw blades for all kinds of things, from jigsaw blades to the big bandsaw blades used in the lumber mills. Today they were announcing a $500,000 investment in new equipment, which would mean another 40 new jobs. Good news in an area that badly needed it.

I walked in just as the president stepped away from the podium. The MP was up next, so I took notes and tried to read the press release. I was going to have to corner the prez after to see what he had to say.

"I saw your story this morning about that kid," he said after the interview. "Do you really think Stubby Booker had anything to do with it?"

This was puzzling.

"Well, I don't know. I imagine the cops will look at that as a possibility. But I really couldn't say for sure."

"But you basically said so in your story."

"I what?"

Just then the MP interrupted to say goodbye, and the president drifted off into the crowd, shaking hands and chatting up whoever he met. Meanwhile I was left standing there, wondering what in hell that was all about.

I figured it out about 15 minutes later when I got to the office and picked up the paper. According to the story, I obviously thought Booker had something to do with it. Bankroft had embellished my story, sticking in the Stubby Booker line I had already decided to leave out. I was pissed.

Every aspiring reporter likes to think how precious their stories are. In fact even the bad writers like to think that the words they spill out should somehow be carved in stone. How they put their heart and soul into making it all just right. It brings on a real sense of being holier than thou, and that no one has the right to change even one syllable.

But of course once you get into the real world and an editor starts re-jigging your stories this attitude is forced to change. At first it can be traumatic, seeing your words rearranged like that. In time you get used to it, and if your editor is any good you eventually accept the fact that what they did makes your stuff sound better. I had reached that point.

But this was different. He hadn't made my story better, he had added shit that didn't belong.

"Where in hell does he get off adding shit to my story, making it look like I'm accusing the local thug of having some guy murdered?" I ranted at Steve Farnham, who had just come in from a meeting with the Massey Vanier high school football coach. Farnham didn't seem to get what I was pissed about.

"We all pretty much figured he ordered the guy dead," Farnham said. "Didn't you?"

"Of course I thought about it. But I have nothing to even confirm the police think he's a suspect. As far as I know one of my stories has gone and accused someone of murder. Someone who may be innocent."

"Look, Bankroft has done this to all of us at one time or another. You just have to live with it."

"Fuck that," I said. End of conversation.

Bankroft showed up about an hour later, and I was ready to make a scene. Everyone from advertising to production heard what I had to say.

"Where in the hell do you get off using my story to accuse someone of murder?"

Bankroft had obviously been in a few of these scraps before, and he was ready for it.

"That little shit was Booker's hired help. I just pointed out the obvious," he said.

"You have no right to accuse someone of murder like that, especially when my name is on it," I said. "You're going to get us sued. Again, I might add."

By now the whole plant was quiet. Casual conversations in advertising had halted, while the typists in production stopped feeding in the wire news.

"Excuse me, but just who in hell do you think your talking to?" Bankroft said, his voice a little higher, a little closer to hysteria.

"I think I'm talking to an editor with a shitty sense of right and wrong who's gone and fucked with my story," I said. I was geared up, I wanted him to explode. I wanted him to lose it and take a swing at me. Though it probably would have hurt like hell if he'd smacked me in my freshly-bruised face.

"Get out of here," he said. "You've got the rest of the week off, and no money to enjoy it. Take your sense of self-righteousness home and wallow in it for a few days. And don't you ever, ever question me again or your ass is outta here."

"Asshole," I said, grabbing my jacket and walking out of the door.

Needless to say I didn't feel quite as tough on the way home. I'd nearly been fired, probably pissed off the boss enough to make sure I was passed over at raise time, and rent was due next week.

To top it all off the Falcon decided to drop its muffler as I crossed the train tracks on the Adamsville Road. I pulled over and used an old coat hanger I had in the trunk to wire it up. I'd see if I could do more later.

That evening I got a call from George Brown, the publisher.

"Take tomorrow off, then come back," Brown said.

"What about Bankroft?"

"Between you and me, I had a little talk with him. He was out of line, and shouldn't have been adding stuff to your story. That's the type of stuff that made us the Granby Liar."

"Look, I just want to do my job right and not get sued."

"Don't worry, we have a guy for that and insurance if things get nasty. We pay a fortune for it because of the last couple of times, and we really can't afford to have it happen again."

The upshot of it all was that I got a day off without pay instead of the week, my penance for bad mouthing the boss in front of everyone. On the condition that I not mention Brown's phone call, or that Bankroft had gotten his wrist slapped.

"When you go back to work, just pretend that nothing happened."

13

That night I slept fitfully, my slumber filled with a jumble of nonsensical images. But it was still more restful than the previous couple of nights. The next morning broke sunny and cool, with a slight breeze from the north. In the distance I could hear the faint honking of geese, some of the first to begin making their way south.

In the injury department I was healing up nicely. The blood had started to dissipate from my eye, and the swelling on the side of my face had begun to subside. The ribs were still a little sore, but livable. I took the bandage off of the cut on my face, figuring it was time to let it air out.

I was faced with a day off, but it wasn't as if I had nothing to do. The lawn needed mowing and the Falcon needed muffler work. Seeing as a new muffler was out of the question, I was going to have to improvise.

"So what will your punishment be, oh mouthy journalist?" Jen asked.

"I thought the best punishment would be to spend the day on the couch eating chips. But barring that maybe I'll fix the car or mow the lawn."

"And when you go back to work?"

"I'll shut my mouth and pretend nothing happened," I said. It was a coached reply, coming out of the discussion we'd had at the dinner table last night. While Jen said she understood my point, she also made it clear that she thought I should have held my temper. Jen had held several crappy jobs, and seemed able to put up with just about anything.

"If you want to get a career going, you're going to have to put up with it," she reminded me over our morning coffee. "It's not like they can't find a replacement, and it's not like you're going to be there forever. You can tell the boss whatever you want the day you leave."

Though I knew she had my best interests at heart, I still felt like she was telling me that I was going to have to eat shit. My only comfort was the knowledge that George Brown had doled out at least a partial helping to Bankroft.

Twenty minutes later Jen's ride showed up, and she was gone to work for the day. She had 30 hours a week now, and it was making a real difference in terms of the money thing. We were still broke, but at least we weren't quite as desperate as we had been. We even had a steak dinner recently.

Left alone with King, I put on my best dirty clothes and headed for the back yard. There was an embankment there I thought could come in handy for my muffler repair job.

After sizing things up and then backing the rear of the Falcon over to the edge of the embankment, I blocked off the wheels. The rear of the car now stood about a foot higher off of the ground than normal. Not exactly an optimal place for a repair job, but there seemed to be enough room to get under there.

Next it was on to the custom repair job. One Molson can (drained the previous weekend), cut to the appropriate size, and put in place with two hose clamps. It stopped about 90 per cent of the leak, and the muffler wasn't going to fall off again anytime soon. To be on the safe side I used a fresh coat hanger for a little extra support.

"Whatcha doin?" a voice asked from the far end of my car. A quick glance showed it was Timmy, a local kid who dropped out of high school a few years back and was still living with his parents.

"Just fixing my car," I said.

Timmy was always around, and we would often see him wandering the streets at all hours of the night. He was harmless and not very bright. But he loved to get all of the gossip in town. He didn't speak a word of French, so his gossip was confined to the English community, of which there were about 25 of us in Brigham.

"So I read that you think Stubby Booker ordered that guy killed," he said. As I stood up I noticed that he was already wearing a winter jacket, even though it wasn't really that cold.

"I didn't say that, not exactly," I said. I suspected that he couldn't even read, and was probably repeating what he had been told. I was trying to keep my answers short, hoping he'd go away. Even King was trying to ignore him. Smart dog.

"But that's what you said, isn't it?" he asked.

"Not exactly. My boss put in the mention of how Simson said Booker's name in court. The story didn't exactly come out and accuse him of anything."

Here I was defending a story that I was still pissed off about. But I also figured the gossip might as well get around that I did not suspect Stubby. Might as well start with the source of the gossip in Brigham, plant the seed, and see what grows.

"We don't really know what happened yet," I continued. "For all we know he got the wrong guy mad at him."

Timmy laughed, the sound seeming to come out through his nose. I decided to push things a little further.

"I don't see why Simson would have mentioned Booker's name in the first place. He probably never even met the guy. At any rate, I didn't think it was right to mention his name at all."

As Timmy walked off I realized how hollow my words felt. I knew that Stubby had ordered Simson dead. To say I wasn't feeling a little paranoid at that moment would be a lie.

In fact I thought about Simson and Booker the rest of the morning while I mowed the lawn. How could this guy be so well connected that he can have somebody killed in a federal prison, so quickly? Simson had been convicted, and apparently had not been taken seriously when it came to finger pointing. So why make him take a dirt nap? Did Simson really know anything?

My main personal concern was that Booker was going to try to sue me. But the more I thought about it the more I realized that there wasn't much he could do. The story might have pointed a finger, but it was still within the bounds of the legal. The facts were there, simply organized in a way that cast some doubts. Bankroft had tread a very fine line, one that journalists like to dance on regularly.

By the time I finished the lawn my head was throbbing. I hadn't noticed it, but I had been clenching my teeth, thinking about the events of the last few days. The stories of Stubby wiping out anyone who crossed him did anything but provide comfort, and kept creeping back into my thoughts.

As I wheeled the mower across the front yard towards the shed I noticed Timmy talking to someone up the street. I wasn't sure, but I thought I could hear Booker's name being carried on the wind.

***

71

The phone woke me up at 8 a.m. Thursday morning. It was Linda, the newsroom secretary.

"Fernand Dubois wants you to call him. Said he'll only be in the office for the next five minutes, then he'll be gone," she said. I was still getting my head around the idea that she started work so early.

Mornings are not the strong suit of your average reporter. Things have to happen before you can report on them, so work days usually start a little later than your typical job. We then end up working until all hours of the night. I have a friend who works at a paper in Ontario who swears that he got into newspapers so he wouldn't have to get out of bed too early.

I forced myself awake, knowing full well that if I didn't get Dubois before he left the office I might miss something important. Once he was gone I wouldn't be able to reach him until God knows when.

"I've got something that might interest you," Dubois said. "Have you ever covered a pot bust before?"

"As a matter of fact, no I have not," I replied. "But I kind of figured it was the right time of year for it."

Dubois gave me a quick fill in on what was going on. About 30 cops had raided a hippie commune down by the border. Based on an investigation that had lasted most of the summer, the provincials figured out that some of the hippies were taking advantage of their location and American citizenship to haul Townships weed south.

"Off the record I think that's how a lot of these guys manage to make enough money to stay here," Dubois said.

In the 60's and early 70's the Flower Power generation in the States was looking for ways to avoid getting drafted and going to Vietnam. Some went to college to avoid the draft, while others who couldn't afford college, or who wanted to drop out of society entirely left the US, choosing to go elsewhere to build their own brand of Utopia.

South of Sutton, just inside the Quebec border is a little village called Abercorn. Just east of Abercorn there's a little dirt track that was nameless in 1975, but is known today as Waterhouse Road. At the end of the road, within a stones throw of the US border, lived a group of about 30 men and women, most of them in their late teens and early 20's. They grew their own food, established their own rules and lived in exile from a country that was still smarting from its recent defeat in southeast Asia.

Not all of the hippies were draft dodgers. Their girlfriends came along, as did some friends. There were also a few anti-war activists who chose exile as a form of protest rather than stay under the system they reviled. By 1975, some of them had children. In the summer they lived in tents, VW vans and small trailer homes.

In the winter they either left the commune for warmer climes or crowded into an old ramshackle house on the property, property owned by an eccentric Montreal millionaire who quietly supported their efforts at social revolution. Though he owned the farm the hippies called home, they never saw him.

By 9 a.m. I was nursing the Falcon up the steep hill to The Farm, as the sign at the foot of the drive called it. I had already missed the main raid, in which the cops barged-in at 6:30 a.m., catching almost everyone still in their beds.

By the time I arrived police officers and hippies were quietly milling about. The main targets of the raids had been hauled away, as well as a few who didn't have the proper paperwork to be in Canada.

The morning air was crisp, and I pulled my jean jacket a little tighter around me. Overhead the sky was a uniform grey, with no indication that the sun had ever shone before.

A young girl, probably no more than 18 or 19, sat in the open side door of a Dodge van, breast feeding an infant. Mother and baby both seemed oblivious to most or what was going on, and to the tension in the air. Though it was only about 50 degrees, neither of them seemed to notice.

Having lived a little closer to the raid than Dubois, I had beaten him to the scene. This was my little chance to look around before he came in and gave me the official story. I decided to try my luck with the breast-feeding mom.

"Excuse me, I'm with the Granby Leader-Mail, and I was wondering if you could tell me what's been going on here this morning."

"What's the Granby Leader-Mail?" came the response, thick with an accent that seemed more appropriate for a Long Island shopkeeper than a teenaged mother in the Townships.

"It's the local newspaper," I said. "I'm just trying to figure out what was going on here."

She said nothing, taking the next few seconds to change breasts. I hadn't been around breast feeders very much, and I wasn't sure if I should be looking or not. Mom didn't seem to care.

"I was up around 6 this morning, because Star here has been teething. He's been miserable lately, so neither of us has gotten any sleep. I don't think the cold in the van has helped very much either."

"You live alone in this thing?" I asked, wondering what she planned to do for the winter.

"Since Tony left last month. People here take care of me, and I don't really have anyplace better to go. Planning to head south in a few weeks, maybe Philadelphia."

"So what happened this morning?"

"Well, as I said I was up, when these cars all start to pull in with their lights off. I thought it was some guys who came here earlier this year, but then I saw the silhouettes of the flashers. Then all hell broke loose."

"The cops brought dogs with them," she continued while removing junior from the milk bar and placing him on a stack of blankets. The left breast stayed out for awhile, taking in a little of the crisp fall air. She tucked it back in as she continued her narrative.

"They went for the house first, two guys kicking in the front door. At the same time a bunch of others began hitting the outbuildings and the tents. They didn't seem to know that I was living here, so I decided to sit tight and try to keep Star quiet."

"I couldn't believe it. They were dragging people out and tossing them around like rag dolls. Worse than some of those protests at the universities. They dragged Francis out of the house and then two of them started kicking him. Then they stuff him in a van and that's the last I saw of him. They hauled a bunch of them away. Janie, Robbie, Hunter. I still don't know how many they got, or why."

"Did they ever find you?" I asked.

"After about a half hour two pigs began pounding on my door. But they'd started to calm down by then, and stuck to asking questions. Even pigs have their limits, I guess."

"They asked me where I was from, if I was with anyone. They asked me a lot of questions about Tony, said they wanted to know where he was. But there wasn't much I could say." she began rolling a cigarette, expertly spreading out the tobacco on a Vogue paper.

"Then something happened in the house, and they suddenly lost interest in me. They haven't been back since."

She pulled out a wooden match and scratched it down the side of the door frame. She examined the flame for a second, before touching it to the end of the cigarette. She exhaled smoke through her nose, and for some reason it made her look even younger.

I had been scribbling a few notes, trying to figure out what I should ask next. Then something clicked.

"You said you thought it was some guys who had come here earlier this year. Who were they?" I asked.

She paused for a moment, suddenly very interested in the glowing tip of her rollie.

"I'm not sure," came the brief reply. I knew I had hit on something.

"I'm just repeating what you said before. Were you guys raided before?"

There was silence, except for the sound of a police radio coming from a cruiser in the main courtyard. I decided to keep quiet, and see if the silence would be uncomfortable enough to make her speak.

"I don't really know who they are," she said after a painfully long pause. "They came here about a month ago. Showed up early in the morning in two cars. I was asleep when Vinnie came and woke up Tony. They went to talk to these guys. I think there was four of them, but I wasn't really awake."

"What did they talk about?"

"Tony wouldn't say. Said he'd tell me when the time was right. A few days later he took off. Didn't even leave a note. So now it's just me and Star."

I could see a tear forming in the corner of her eye. Here was this girl, God knows how far from home, complete with a baby boy and living alone in a van. Winter was only a couple of months away, and her prospects didn't look good. I found myself feeling a little uncomfortable, not knowing if I should comfort her or just walk away. In the end I wished her well, left her my office number if anything came up, and politely excused myself.

I had just spotted a clean shaven guy with a ponytail and bib overalls and was making my way towards him when Fernand Dubois pulled into the yard. He immediately yelled for me, thus ruining my shot at asking bib overalls a few questions.

Dubois gave me the official line. About 30 cops, most from the Major Crimes division and the Cowansville detachment of the Quebec Police Force had swept down on the commune at 6:30 a.m. They then proceeded to arrest six people and bring them in for questioning. No word yet on if they would actually be charged with anything.

This much was already known: Two of the six were in the country illegally. If they weren't actually charged with anything, they would be escorted to the border.

The raid also turned up about 75 pounds of marijuana buds, which the cops said was worth about $75,000. I was no expert, but I felt reasonably sure that nobody on The Farm was going to see anything near that amount of cash.

According to the findings of the police investigation, residents at The Farm had been growing their own, as well as buying from area growers. They would then haul the stuff through the woods across the border. From there it was handed off to a US connection.

"We first learned about it when we got a call from the Vermont State Troopers," Dubois said. "In case you hadn't noticed it's pretty remote here, and we didn't even know these hippies were living here."

The State Troopers apparently found out by accident, stopping a pickup truck for a routine road check. The back was filled with garbage bags full of pot. The driver got scared and spilled the beans. He was now headed for a state pen, looking at three to five years.

"Do you know who they were buying the stuff from?" I asked.

"I can't really say right now, but the investigation is continuing," came the coy reply.

"Is this part of a larger operation?"

"Once again I can't really say at this time."

"Are you expecting to make further arrests?"

"We don't know yet."

It was quickly becoming clear that Dubois had said all he was going to. I said thanks and began to wander off.

Bib overalls was now sitting on a gate near the barn by now, still quietly surveying the scene. Figuring I had nothing to lose, I decided to ask him a few questions. I introduced myself and he quietly shook my hand.

"Did you see the raid this morning?" I began.

"Yeah, don't want to talk about it much though," came the reply. He seemed distracted, like his mind was on something else.

"I'm just trying to figure out what's happening here," I responded. "I'd like to get both sides of the story."

"Well, my side of it is that I was fast asleep when all of a sudden there's cops everywhere. As if things weren't hairy enough around here, outsiders messing up everything."

"Hairy enough?"

"What?" the distracted reply.

"You said 'As if things weren't hairy enough.'"

Silence. The distracted look was replaced by a look of intense thought, maybe concern.

"I think I'm done talking for now," he said.

"Well, just in case you feel like talking again sometime, here's my card. If I'm not there they can usually find me fairly quickly."

He took my card without a word, stuffing it in the chest pocket of the bib overalls. I suddenly realized I hadn't gotten his name.

"I didn't get your name," I said as he jumped off of the fence and began to walk away.

"Probably better that way," his back replied.

14

The raid on the hippie commune made for a good story. I talked to Fernand Dubois late in the day and he confirmed that two of the six arrested were being sent back to the States, while three of the four others nabbed in the raid were going to be charged in court tomorrow for various crimes related to growing, smuggling and selling marijuana.

Because they hadn't yet been charged with anything, the cops weren't going to give me their names. With deadline only a few hours away, that part of the story would have to wait.

Bankroft ran the story on front, above the fold, continued on page 3. Inside the story was accompanied by a photo of a cop with a note pad questioning a hippie, taken by a freelancer later in the day. I don't know if I was getting better, or if Bankroft was going easy on me after our little brawl. Either way, the story ran verbatim.

I was still feeling a little vindicated by lunchtime Friday when Jen showed up at the office. She had ended up with an unexpected afternoon off and had managed to wrangle a ride to Granby and wanted to go out for lunch. We headed for one of the little coffee shops across from the courthouse. Along the way we talked casually about her ride, one of her weaver's guild friends who had decided to come to Granby for the day to do some shopping.

After settling in with a couple of cups of coffee, soups and sandwiches, it became apparent that something was on Jen's mind. I decided to cut to the chase and ask her outright.

"Well, I was working at the library this morning, shelving books. Just as I was tucking a copy of Never Cry Wolf back onto one of the shelves, this other book, only a foot or so away, gets pushed off the shelf by someone from the next aisle."

"It didn't really click on me at first, so I just bent over and picked it up," she continued. "Then another couple of books fell, just missing my head."

"'What are you doing?' I asked, even though I still couldn't see who it was. For a second I thought it might be you, trying to mess with my head."

"Then I saw this big arm come through the shelf as he shoved another half dozen books onto the floor. I walked around the end of the aisle and the guy, whoever he was, was quickly walking towards the door. I went after him, but he picked up the pace, and got outside before I could reach him. I called out a few times, but he just ignored me and kept walking."

"By the time I got to the door he was getting into a blue car, I think it was a Valiant, and someone drove him away," she finished. "It scared the hell out of me."

"Did you get a look at the guy at all?" I asked, a feeling of worry creeping into the pit of my stomach.

"All I could see was from behind. He was wearing a long black trench coat that looked too big for him. He had curly hair, almost like an afro. That's it."

"Anyways, I went back to the stacks to clean up the mess this guy left me. Nothing like this had ever happened before, so I was feeling a little unnerved. Then I found this note on the floor with the books."

She produced a piece of loose leaf paper, the kind kids use in school. In large block letters written in black marker were the following words:

ROGERS: BACK OFF.

I paused for a moment, letting it all sink in. The worry in my stomach reaching its fingers across my torso. Jen said what I was already beginning to feel.

"Look Dave, I don't think this guy was telling me to back off. I work in the library, do my pottery and dabble in the weaver's guild. What would he want from me, to stop reshelving books?"

"You didn't refuse this guy a library card?" I said in an attempt at a joke that fell flat. The effect was in fact the opposite, with Jen getting a little angry.

"Look, my job might not be the greatest, but I'm not the one in the position to be able to stir up shit, you are. And I have to follow along, because I'm you're wife. Well, I never asked for a visit from afro man."

"I'm sorry. I just don't know what to make of all of this," I said. My mind was whirling unproductively, looking for the right thing to say.

"It's just another thing to make me feel like I'm some kind of accessory to your life," she went on. "You work all kinds of crappy hours, get paid nothing, and are so burnt out when you get home you have nothing to say."

"You know this is just temporary. Until something opens up in the city, then we can go back," I replied, my mind still spinning its wheels in mental mud, trying to figure out if I should keep talking about the man or the issues that were being introduced to the conversation.

"It's not here that I mind, in fact I like it here and think it would be a great place to raise kids. But I'm sick of being poor, of living like a student. When I get harassed by some stranger for you, it makes me feel resentful," she said, her eyes watered, but only for an instant. "I don't like resenting you, and I know all that stuff about your career. But I want to do things too, like having a life with a husband and the freedom to do what we want. I'm just tired of waiting for it."

Money had been one of the main stresses in our relationship. For the most part we had gotten used to living on little, but every now and then one of us would have to bitch about not having enough to do more than get by. The demands of my job and what it did to me also crept back into the conversation.

This time my problems were carried back from the depths by a curly-haired man in a baggy trench coat.

The saving grace in these discussions was that at the core of it all we shared similar values. We both wanted to be able to live comfortably, and I didn't want a wife who would simply be an extension of myself. It was Jen's self-assuredness and independent nature that drew me to her in the first place. The problem was balancing that with the driving need to make a name for myself in a business that I was learning seemed to be largely filled with workaholics.

We talked awhile longer, but it was hard to come to a satisfactory conclusion. Jen was still upset about her run-in with afro man, and the other issues were not ones that could simply go away with a few kind words. Still, we knew where we stood, and it seemed we were at least facing the same direction.

We walked back to the office, where Jen was going to hang out until her ride returned. She kept herself busy visiting with Linda, our secretary, and reading through the stacks of newspapers. She didn't even mention the papers mounded up on my desk, looking like a loud noise could trigger an avalanche at any moment.

I made a few calls on stories, but I found my interviews were awkward, filled with halting and not very original questions. My thoughts were more on the ROGERS: BACK OFF note, wondering what it could all mean.

Jen's ride showed up at around 3 p.m., and five minutes later I was on the phone with Fernand Dubois, to see if he had anything to suggest.

"There's not really anything we can do," Dubois said. "You have no idea who he was, or why he sent that note. Hell, you don't even know for sure if it was for you or your wife."

"Look, could you at least make a record of this, in case anything else happens?" I said.

"I can write it down, but I wouldn't count on ever needing it," he said. "I doubt you'll ever see this guy again."

A few minutes later Rachel Porter gave me a pep talk, telling me I had nothing to worry about.

"This kind of thing happens all the time, though this is the first time I've ever heard of them going after a spouse," she said. "People get pissed off and start talking about how they're going to get even. They rant and rave a bull, but that's about it. I've never heard of any of these assholes actually going after someone."

Rachel went on to tell me about a case she covered in court a year earlier. The guy told her that if she wrote anything he'd come after her. Six months later he was out of jail when she saw him at a corner store. He glared at her, but that was the end of it. No problem.

Still, I was having a problem accepting that there was nothing to worry about. I took stock of all of the stories I'd done recently, listing them out and trying to figure out just who would be pissed at me.

First off there was the town councilor in Roxton Pond who wanted to push through a sewage system that was to be installed by his brother in law. But it seemed unlikely he would do anything like that, it just wasn't his style. And besides, it was another councilor who tipped me off, so chances are he'd be higher up on the shit list than me.

Then there was the hippie commune story. Hippies got busted, some people were going to go to jail. Probably there weren't that many of them who read the paper, and even fewer who would care. Unless the people they dealt with were upset, but that didn't add up somehow.

The next possibility was the Mark Simson murder. His mother was probably still mad as hell at me, but her son's story was pretty much over, unless they found his killers. Why would she not want me to report on who killed her son?

That just didn't add up, either.

Simson's killers were on the inside, and not likely to be able to get at me, let alone a copy of the paper. If they were hired by someone on the outside, there most likely wouldn't be anything to prove it, whether I covered it or not.

And just who would have hired them anyways?

Stubby Booker.

But that was a pretty tenuous grasp at best. I still had no evidence that he would have any reason to kill Simson, let alone the connections to be able to hire someone already in prison to do the job.

Even if it was one of Booker's men at the library, what could I do? Not much. Except pack up and move to the unemployment line, which wasn't much of an option.

I even gave myself a little lecture on that last point. Reporting is a high stress job, where conflict is a normal part of the diet. If I quit at the first sign of a threat, I might as well get out of the business.

Still, I hated that they had dragged my wife into this. Give me a fair fight, on even ground. Leave the others out of it.

That night as I lay in bed my mind raced with the implications of Jen's little meeting. But try as I might I couldn't figure it out. Booker was the best candidate, but I still had no evidence to suggest why. My thinking was unproductive, but it still kept me awake.

When I finally did fall asleep my dreams were filled with images of people pursuing me, taking me hostage. A couple of the men in my dreams wore long trench coats and sported Bozo the Clown curly hairdos. I caught a brief image of my father in there somewhere, shaking his head. He didn't say anything, but I knew what he was thinking.

***

After a few days the initial concern over Jen's encounter died down. She even cracked a couple of jokes about it, and it seemed to live less and less in my thoughts. The film loop in my head of a menacing man walking out of the library slowly began to wear thin, then quietly fade from view.

Over the next couple of weeks the Townships literally exploded into colour. The leaves began changing from deep greens to shades of red, yellow and orange. Hills and valleys, impressive to this city boy already, became so spectacular that I regularly found myself pulling the Falcon to the side of the road so I could stop and take it all in. The air felt alive, with a crispness that made drawing every breath feel as if you were doing something wonderful for your body.

Late September was giving way to October, and doing it in style. One afternoon, I think it was a Tuesday, I made myself disappear for about three hours, touring back roads to nowhere. I passed abandoned houses, small family farms that probably looked much as they had for the last several generations, and tar paper shacks that looked like they wouldn't be able to survive a strong wind. In between there were large tracts of mesmerizing forests, bedecked in orange and yellow. Occasionally the greens of conifers filled out the palate.

I strolled back into the office around 4:30, expecting to have to come up with an excuse for why no one had been able to find me. No one asked, and with not a lot to do I typed up my morning assignment and left around 6.

It was a good day.

The following morning, refreshed from a solid night's sleep, I actually made it in to work for 9 a.m. I was also feeling a little guilty about playing hooky yesterday, so I wanted to get an early start on things. The bright sunshine of the previous day had been replaced by a solid sheet of grey clouds.

By the time I walked in the door Linda our secretary was in the process of phoning Rachel to get her out of bed. The cops had found a body, and she needed to find a reporter. I volunteered before she could complete the call.

"One of our readers, an old guy with a police scanner, said he heard the cops talking about it an hour ago. Up on Miltimore Road, not far from Cowansville."

I had in fact been on a Miltimore Road during my back road odyssey, but it turned out that there was more than one road in the region with that same name. I dug out my map, found the road in question with a little help from Linda, and loped out the door.

I considered calling Dubois to get the lowdown first. But I figured that might make the difference between being able to do some questioning at the scene of the crime and arriving after the last cop car had faded into the distance. I opted to get over there fast, and worry about Dubois later.

A quick tour up Pierre Laporte, past Bromont. Left on Gaspé Road, and right on to Miltimore. I had arrived at my first murder scene.

I had expected to see lots of yellow crime scene tape and police cars strewn about with their flashers on. What I saw instead was one cruiser, two unmarked cars and a white van with the Quebec Police Force's trademark yellow doors.

Feeling a combined rush of dread and excitement I stepped out of the Falcon and went to see. So far, I was the only non-police person there, save for the deado.

Dubois wasn't even here yet, so I talked to a detective named Peterson. Despite the English name he spoke with a heavy French accent. I offered to switch to French, but he continued in English anyway.

"Old man went for walk dis morning, saw some'ting in da water," he said. "We been here since 7:30."

Peterson wasn't much on the information, slowed by his poor English. But since I was the only reporter around, he did let me get a glimpse of the action.

Miltimore Road dips down as it comes to one of the thousands of nameless brooks that wend their way through the Townships. The bridge was barely wide enough for two small cars to pass each other, and the guardrails were made of squared timbers soaked in creosote.

As the old man crossed the bridge he looked down and saw something in a pool of water about three feet deep. Leaning over the rail it was easy to tell that it was a dead body. The killers were probably banking that people rarely walked on this remote back road, giving them better chances that it would be awhile before the discovery.

As I leaned over the rail the waterlogged and slightly fishy smell of the body met my nostrils. The officers were still combing the area, and still hadn't moved the corpse from its temporary watery grave.

Looking back on it the thing I remember the most is how I horrified I wasn't at the sight of the murdered man, the first I'd ever seen. Maybe it was the sight of a half dozen police officers milling about, visiting casually, as if everything was normal. The body, while obviously human, almost didn't seem real. It looked more like a discarded cocoon. A human had lived there once, but had moved on to something else.

Hopefully something better.

The officers were systematically combing the surrounding area, looking for anything that could help. An empty shell casing, some clothing, even a foot print or a sign of a struggle.

If I'd been Sherlock Holmes, this would have been the point at which I told the cops that they were trampling on valuable evidence. I would have gone on to point to a scuff mark on a tree, or perhaps a flake of blue paint. From this I would have been able to wow the assembled police officers with a detailed account of the final few moments of the man's life.

"The killer is a stocky man who walks with a limp. He seems to have been wearing military issue combat boots, which he used to great effect on the victim."

Instead, I stood on the bridge, noticed nothing that hadn't been seen already, and let the cops do their jobs.

About 20 minutes later two police officers in hip waders stepped into the brook and rolled the man over. He had brown hair that covered his ears, and smashed spectacles, like the ones John Lennon wore, still on his face.

He wore a leather vest with some brightly coloured beads on it. The vest was open in the front, and from my vantage point I could clearly see three round holes in his chest.

The body was rigid, with one arm clutching his chest and the other sticking straight out to the side. A police photographer snapped two photos, then the body was carried to the bank. A body bag was unrolled on the ground nearby, and what remained of the apparently young man was placed in it.

The arm refused to go into the bag. Until a man in a white lab coat rolled the body onto its side, with the arm pointing to the slate grey sky, and put his knee on it. With an audible cracking sound the arm swung down and touched the side of the body. The bag was zipped shut. The man made a comment I couldn't hear, and a police officer nearby laughed uncomfortably.

Would these men have been so nonchalant if it had been me? Probably, but I didn't want to think about it too much.

"We tink de body's been dere for a few days, au moins," Peterson said. "We know more later."

"Any idea who he is?" I asked.

"Non. We know more later."

With our photographer nowhere in sight, I got the camera from my car, and took a few pictures. Police officer putting something into a plastic bag. The body being loaded into the van with the yellow doors. The two cops with the hip waders now examining the pool of water for clues.

Just then I spotted an old man in a flannel jacket on the road. He stayed at a distance, surveying the scene while puffing on a short, fat cigar. Snow white hair stuck out from under an orange baseball hat, with white sideburns sweeping down to the corners of his mouth.

Peterson approached the man, and the two spoke in French. I couldn't hear what was said, but the conversation was short. Peterson had other things to do.

Figuring this was probably the guy who found the body, I decided to go ask some questions. I think the old boy saw me coming with my camera and my notepad. I barely had time to identify myself.

"Go cause trouble with someone else," he said in French.

"I'm just trying to figure out what happened here," I replied in French.

"I understand, but I didn't want to find this guy and I don't want my name in your paper," he replied in flawless English. "Do your job, just don't do it with me."

Figuring that he wouldn't be able to tell me much more than I already knew, I let it drop. He wouldn't have been able to give me more than a little colour for the story anyways.

It began to rain, so I went back to my car and waited awhile longer. Dubois never showed up, and neither did our photographer. When the van pulled away to take the body to the morgue, I decided it was time to head back to the office.

I drove slowly on the trip back, trying to take in what I had just seen. I'd never seen a dead body before, except at a funeral. The total lack of horror by myself or anyone else there was a little disconcerting, like I'd missed something.

I was back at the office by 11 o'clock. I had the background for the story, but few real details. I called Dubois to see what he knew. But Dubois was sick, so I spoke to the duty officer. He didn't have much for me to go on, and suggested I call at the end of the day, after he had the chance to talk to his investigators.

At least it was a Wednesday, so I still had a day before deadline. With a little luck they'd have him I.D.'d, and maybe even a little background info.

The rest of that day was spent on other matters, including a story on a new x-ray machine at the Granby Hospital. The photographer made it to that one.

That night I went home, made love to my wife and slept soundly. No images of bodies floating in brooks, no thoughts about the nameless man's last few hours in this world.

15

"His name is Anthony Bakerstein, an American," the voice at the other end of the line told me Thursday morning.

It was Dubois, back at work, though he sounded terrible. His words were forced through a filter of phlegm by badly strained vocal cords. I could almost feel the heat of his fever through the phone line.

"He had identification on him, including a driver's licence from Rhode Island," Dubois continued. "We're trying to figure out why he was here in the first place."

Normally Dubois would only answer the questions that I asked him, making me work for it. It was part of the little head games he liked to play with reporters. But today, weakened by illness, he wasn't in the mood for games. Instead he was giving me the information he had, and I didn't even have to ask questions.

"We still don't have much to go on, but the Major Crimes Squad is on it. We know from his wallet that he was 23 years old, and listed Rhode Island as his address. He was shot three times at close range in the chest, most likely at or near the scene."

"Ballistics tests will tell us for sure, but the shots appear to have come from a handgun. As you know Bakerstein's body was then dumped into the brook."

"How long had he been there?" I asked.

"Probably a week or two, though we're still waiting to hear more from the coroner. We should know more later today," the voice croaked to a halt. A fit of coughing followed it.

"Why in hell did you come in to work today?" I asked. "You sound like shit."

"They wanted me in for this," he replied. "The duty officer doesn't like talking to the press."

"I'll call back later. In the meantime go get some rest," I said.

I spent the next few minutes going over my notes. Anthony Bakerstein. Probably Jewish, apparently from Rhode Island. Anthony.... Tony.

Tony, the guy who ran off and left the little hippie girl and their newborn child?

It made sense.

The hippie clothes and John Lennon specs. The US citizenship, just like the ones that got busted. A reason for why he was in the area, probably a draft dodger. A reason why he left his woman with no warning and no goodbyes.

I pictured her, still sleeping in the van with a newborn child. Probably wondering why Tony dumped her. Family and the usual support systems most of us have would be far away. She probably was hoping he'd return, complete with a good explanation that would make all of the hurt and loneliness disappear. Return with a plan to keep her and her son from freezing to death this winter in the back of a Dodge van.

It didn't seem like that was going to happen now.

I pondered the idea of calling Dubois back to let him know about my hunch. Usually I wouldn't want to help the cops do their jobs. I was a reporter, just there as an impartial observer, letting others take action while I watched.

Then I pictured Anthony Bakerstein's bullet-ridden body. If he was Tony, then his son was now orphaned by a man with whom he shared genetic makeup, but who he would never know. Then again, I could be wrong.

Dubois answered the phone on the third ring in the middle of a coughing fit.

"Listen," I said, "When I was out at the hippie commune I spoke with a young girl who had a boyfriend named Tony. She said he just took off one day, God knows where."

I gave Dubois the gist if the interview, making it clear that all I really knew was that there was a guy named Tony who used to live at The Farm.

"She also said that when you guys arrived the other morning she thought it was, as she put it, 'the guys who came here earlier this year.'"

There was a pause at the other end of the line. I heard some papers being shuffled.

"Did she say who 'the guys' were?" Dubois asked.

"Wouldn't say any more than that."

"She told you all of that and wouldn't tell you anything else?"

I knew I had his attention.

"Sorry, nothing. She changed the subject after that."

"Nothing?"

"Nothing."

"Well, it probably is nothing, but I'll pass it on to the investigators, see what they have to say. Do you mind if they call you back?"

"They can call me all they want," I said. "But honestly, I've told you all I know. I never got to dig any further."

"Well, thanks for this," Dubois said.

"Look, if this turns out to be something, I want you to call me. I think I at least deserve a good story out of it. And holding off on the others wouldn't be a bad idea either."

Dubois agreed, and then erupted into another coughing fit. He sounded so sick I doubted he'd even be able to make it down the hall to tell the detectives. At any rate, if it led to the girl finding out what happened to her beloved beau, then that was all I really cared about at this point. Getting a good story lead or maybe even a scoop would be a nice bonus, though.

It being Thursday, I was going to have to write up what I had. Murders are pretty rare in the Townships, so I was pretty much assured of a page one story.

At 3 o'clock I called Dubois, but got no answer. Probably gone home to bed, with nothing to offer on what I'd given him.

I told it straight, giving only the facts I knew for sure. An old man out for a walk found a body, who police identified as one Anthony Bakerstein of Rhode Island. Shot three times, dumped in a brook. No known reason why he was here, or why he was shot. A little colour about the investigators combing the scene, etc, etc. I decided to leave out the bit about the rigor mortis arm.

When you tell a crime story like this, and there aren't any interviews with witnesses or victims, it doesn't take long. I ended up with about 300 words, tapped out on the Underwood.

At around 4:30 I was just giving it a last look over before handing it off to Bankroft when the phone rang. It was Dubois.

"How would you like a job as a cop?" he sounded excited.

"No thanks, they're all pricks," I said, without really thinking, and immediately cringing.

"Your story worked out," he went on as if he didn't hear it. "We sent a car over to The Farm and it turns out that Tony is Anthony. Girl took it pretty hard, too."

"So is there any connection with the pot smugglers and his death?" I asked.

"We don't know. They don't like to talk to us much since we busted their friends. We had a hard enough time getting them to admit that Tony even lived there."

"Anything else?" I asked, already thinking about how I'd rejig my story.

"The coroner says the body had been there about ten days. The cold water helped to keep him preserved. And he was shot with a handgun, probably a .38."

"Have you told anyone else?" my final question.

"No time, this is as fresh as it gets."

With this information I was going to have to change what I'd already written. But there wasn't enough time to rewrite the whole thing. It was time to break out the scissors.

First, I took the original story and cut out the parts that I wouldn't have to rewrite, namely the details about the scene of the crime. The lead was thrown in the trash bin.

From there I had to come up with a new lead: "The body of a man found shot in Bromont on Tuesday has been identified as that of an American citizen."

Second paragraph gave Bakerstein's name and the few details we had about him: He was from Rhode Island, and had been living at the hippie commune with his girlfriend and newborn son. He was shot three times in the chest at close range, most likely with a .38 revolver.

Taped on to the page after that were the paragraphs from the original, explaining how the body was found, and details of the scene.

From there it was back to the new stuff: The police still had no idea why he was shot, or by whom. More questions would be asked at the commune. Mention of the earlier raid at the commune in connection with a drug smuggling operation. Leave that one hanging, to imply that the smuggling and the shooting were connected, without actually saying so. A bit like the way Bankroft stuck Booker's name into the mark Simson murder.

Forty-five minutes later I handed Bankroft an 800 word story, cobbled together from the old and the new. He grunted at the sight of the taped papers, but accepted it anyways. He knew and missed the daily thrills of life at the Montreal Star, and this was as close to deadline rushing exclusive news as he was able to get these days.

Five minutes later he had his red pen out, doing his best to make the story not read like it had been put together from bits and pieces. Two cigarettes later he sent it off to the typist.

I gave it a look over while the typist was working on another story. I was still a bit peeved with my boss, but I had to reluctantly admit he made it all flow a little better.

"Not a bad bit of work," Bankroft said from his desk, taking a pause from editing copy. He was in fact procrastinating to let things build a little more before deadline. Gotta build the rush.

"Are you sure we got the scoop on this?" he said as I walked over and sat on the couch next to his desk.

"As far as I know. I scratched their backs on this one, on the condition that they give me the story," I replied. I explained how I had a hunch that I passed on to the cops, and it paid off.

"I wouldn't make a habit of that," Bankroft said, pausing for a drag on his Export A. "You got something out of it this time, but you don't want to be doing their jobs for them. It's a fine line, and they aren't necessarily your friends."

I glanced around to see if the others were hearing this. Rachel Porter was rattling away on her Selectric, while John McAuslan and Steve Farnham were apparently both deeply into their stories.

"There isn't much in the book for tomorrow," Bankroft said. "Come in here in the morning and see what's going on. If things are looking quiet by lunch, head over and pay the hippies a visit. See what they have to say about all of this."

16

It was the first Friday in October, but it felt almost like a Sunday.

The morning was cool, with the faded 7 Up thermometer nailed to the side of our house reading a scant 50 degrees in the morning sun. By noon things would warm up to 60 or a little higher. There was talk of the government bringing in the Metric System, bringing Canada more in line with much of the rest of the world. But the real world of 1975 was still firmly run on miles an hour, pounds, ounces and miles to the gallon. Degrees Fahrenheit.

Breakfast was the usual quick affair, with neither Jen nor I being big breakfast eaters. Especially on a work day, when there wasn't time to sit back and relax afterwards.

I threw on my jean jacket and stepped into the fresh fall air. The temperature had dipped to near freezing last night, and the bench seat of the Falcon was a little harder than usual.

The leaves were still in full colour, lining des Érables out of Brigham with hues of orange and red. As I approached a tree-lined hill I was met by a burly man on a red International with a front end loader, a plow swaying gently on the back as he worked his way down the hill. He didn't really look anything like him, but this farmer made me think of my father. The sadness of loss hit for a few seconds, before I managed to push it back to its normal resting place.

Work seemed to be the last thing on anybody's mind at the office. In between the ringing of the phones sales reps gossiped about the day's headlines. Towards the back a couple of the pressmen were talking loudly in French about the coming hunting season. Steve Farnham and John McAuslan had their feet up on their desks.

I was of two minds about my workday. Bankroft had said that if things were quiet I could go out to The Farm and nose around. That could be interesting, particularly if there was fodder out there for a story. But then again they might not take kindly to me nosing around, with one of their own dead and all.

So on one hand I could make myself busy and avoid the whole thing, but on the other that might mean passing up a really good follow-up. I did what I usually do in these situations: I procrastinated, shuffling papers while the back of my mind shuffled possibilities.

By 11 it was becoming obvious that nothing else was going to come up to occupy my time. It seemed that the rest of the world was into the Friday thing, taking it easy until they could escape for the weekend.

Being on the road helped my frame of mind, the sunshine pushing out any negative thoughts. Pierre Laporte Road meandered along the side of Mount Brome, the Falcon purring along on all six cylinders. I cracked the window open and turned up the radio. Cat Stevens.

My last visit to the Sutton region had been on a grey, overcast day. But today's sunshine transformed the mountains into a breathtaking palette of colours, the likes of which I don't think I'd ever seen before. To this day the stunning beauty of the colours surprises me every fall.

The town of Sutton fits well with its surroundings. It's a sleepy little town that could have just as easily been slipped into any valley in New England. It has just the right level of tranquility and quiet dustiness.

Abercorn is half the size and just as sleepy. I cruised by the Prince of Wales Hotel and into the Missisquoi Valley, then turned down the dirt track that led to The Farm. The track then climbed a steep hillside, winding up into the foothills of the Sutton Mountains.

At about this point the dread started to set back in. I was going into the unknown, where the outcome could be good or bad. I clenched my gut and pressed a little harder on the accelerator.

Pulling into the large open yard, I parked the car as far away from the main house as I could.

Shutting off the car I spent a few seconds getting things in order. The notepad was tucked in the rear waistband of my pants, covered by my T-shirt and jean jacket. I pulled out the tail of the shirt and did the best I could to look like I belonged there. Or at least didn't look like a narc.

Under a sprawling maple about a hundred yards from the house I saw the familiar Dodge van, and decided this was the best place to start.

"How's it going?" I asked the girl as I walked up.

"Getting by," came the short reply. Her eyes were red as she gently rocked her sleeping son. Two days ago she was a single mom wondering where her boyfriend had run off to. Yesterday she found out what happened, and was still wishing it would all just go away.

"I heard about Tony," I said, suddenly feeling even more awkward than I had before. I should have known better than to approach the grieving widow right off.

"He was just looking to make a few bucks," she said, staring off towards the mountains. "Said he had a plan that would get us through the winter. I was so mad at him when he just took off like that. I thought maybe he'd found someone else. Now I wish he had."

"Did you have any idea what was going on?" I asked, deciding to plunge on with my questioning.

"I knew he was running across the border, that's all. He didn't say much more than that. I didn't like it, but we were broke. He said he was going to take care of it all."

Her words were robotic, devoid of emotion. It didn't take a long look to be able to tell she was running on shock, not yet fully grasping the horror of what had happened to Tony. The thousand mile stare said things she still could not.

Not sure of the best course of action, I pushed on.

"You said before something about some guys who had come here before. Do you know who they were?"

"They were the guys Tony and the others were working for. It was easy work, just run it through the woods. I never talked to them."

"I didn't like it, but we didn't have much choice," she went on. "We need to eat. We need a place to stay for the winter. I want to go home."

The tears were flowing freely down her cheeks now. She began to shake. I wanted to comfort her, but I was a stranger. A stranger stirring things up. I could feel the wave of grief that was now washing over her body.

I stood there watching a girl who, in her rush to grow up, had turned her back on the things she now desperately craved. Shattered by events she didn't fully understand. Shattered by three slugs planted in the chest of the man who was supposed to take care of things.

I wished I'd found something better to do at the office. I began looking for a graceful way to flee back to my car. But there wasn't really anything I could do.

I decided to back off on the details of Tony's plans. Instead I danced delicately around what she was going to do. She wanted to go back home, but was scared. How would her parents handle their unmarried daughter and her infant son? How could she swallow the pride that carried her away from home in the first place?

She placed her sleeping son on a pile of blankets in the van before casually rolling a cigarette. She offered me one, but I turned it down. I was never a smoker, but at that point it almost seemed like a good idea.

Off near a gate I spotted Mr. Bib Overalls. He was watching us, not moving or speaking. Motionless like a statue, observing like he had been the other day. I suspect he was ready to step in if it looked like I was harassing her too much.

"Here's my number if you need to talk or anything," I said, handing her my business card. I immediately felt like I was overstepping my bounds, a married man making a pass at a widow. What would I say if she did call? How in hell could I, a complete stranger, help her out? Like it would do anything more than make both of us feel awkward.

I wished I was elsewhere. Preferably in a bar somewhere, nursing a quart of Labatt's 50 and thinking about anything but The Farm and its residents. Maybe watching a football game on a big TV bolted to the wall. Alouettes vs. the Hamilton Tiger Cats.

I excused myself and decided to approach Mr. Bib Overalls again. He made no move to avoid my gaze or walk away. Passive. A hairy hippie carved in stone and decked out in denim.

"Feel like talking anymore?" I asked. I knew he remembered me, remembered talking about how outsiders had been messing things up for them.

"Nice day isn't it?" came the reply, no emotion.

"I guess you know about the murder," I said. "I'm just trying to figure out what's going on. What it all means."

"Some things are better left in the dark," he said. "Tony didn't seem to understand that."

"Was it something to do with the smuggling?" I asked.

"No comment."

"Is there anything you can tell me?"

"No," he said, staring off towards the woods.

"Is there anyone here who would like to talk to me about this?"

"You'd best let this be," he said, and started to walk off. "There are a lot of angry people around here. We've been busted and one of our people has been murdered. It's not supposed to be what we are about. This wasn't supposed to happen."

I took his point. Besides not wanting to be dragged into the whole Vietnam thing, these people were looking to build their own little world. A world without killing and without the cops harassing them. They were searching to create the embodiment of the hippie ideal.

Now, rocked by a murder and under the scrutiny of the police, the world that was just out of their grasp seemed further away than ever. They were responding by withdrawing from society, hoping that by doing so they could pull it all back together. A sense of innocence had been lost, and they were too bewildered to even begin to know where to look for it.

From their perspective it was society that was at fault. I had the feeling that I was seen by them as a part of that society. I was closed out.

"You have my card if you change your mind," I said.

I walked back to the car, deciding to take his advice and not dig any further for now. Chances are the others would respond in the same way. Some of them might not be so polite. It's exhausting being an interloper.

As I eased the Falcon back down the hill I thought over what I had just heard. Would I be able to weave a story out of it? Was there anything there that was usable? Still no idea who the shooter was, or how it all tied together.

I stopped at a phone booth in Sutton and called Dubois. I didn't mention the visit to The Farm, but wanted to know if there were any new developments. Something to thread it all together. There was nothing new, so he fed me the standard "The investigation is continuing," line.

Shit.

I kept driving, deciding then and there to head back home instead of driving all the way back to Granby, only to call the work week over an hour later. I'd stop by Racine's along the way and pick up a six-pack to put the week on ice. Or maybe a 12-pack, like the old days.

It was during the drive home I figured I could squeeze a few inches of text out of my visit. A short piece on how residents at the hippie colony were handling the trauma of being raided and losing one of their own. I could use a few quotes from the widow, and maybe one comment from Bib Overalls. Perhaps the bit about "This wasn't supposed to happen."

That evening, buoyed by the glow of three Labatt 50's, I sat at the kitchen table and scrawled out a quick version in longhand, a sympathetic portrait of people in mourning. I'd clean it up at the typewriter Monday.

A half-dozen beers after that and Jen was gently leading me to bed. It had been awhile since I'd had more than one or two, and it hit me hard. I stuck my leg out from under the covers and placed my foot on the floor, to stop the room from spinning. Then I fell into a dark and mercifully dreamless sleep.

17

The next morning dawned a little brighter than I would have liked, the sun blazing into our bedroom and burning holes in my skull. My mouth was full of sand and my foot was still on the floor. I don't think I moved all night.

Jen was still asleep, so I quietly made my way to the bathroom and our supply of Aspirin. A side trip to the kitchen where I poured myself a large glass of water, taking several gulps before letting King out to commune with nature.

The water hit my stomach pretty hard. So this is why I don't drink anymore, I thought.

I flipped on the TV and then settled on to the couch, the volume low. Nothing else to do but wait for the Aspirin to kick in. My hair hurt.

TV consisted of the Pink Panther. What the hell, it's Saturday.

As Blue, the aardvark, was using his bottle of Instant Hole to get that damned red ant, I noticed my story lying on the coffee table. A quick read was enough to show my slowly clearing head that a rewrite was in order. Hemingway could write great literature when he was drunk. Apparently I could not.

Actually, in terms of literature it wasn't so bad. In terms of a news story it was dreadful. All sense of impartiality, a trait I prided myself on, had gone out the window. Replaced by soppy prose telling of a people who set out to build utopia, only to have it savagely destroyed by a society that wanted to keep them down.

To say it was a little over the top would be putting it mildly. The six sheets of loose leaf quickly found their way to the trash.

"So there's the great writer himself," said Jen, poking her head around the corner from the kitchen. She'd drank more responsibly than I, and seemed to be in the mood to tease me.

"How big is your head this morning?" she asked.

"I had to turn sideways to get through the door," I replied.

"To think you tried to jump me last night."

"I did?"

"Yes you did lover boy, but you wanted me to do all the work. You

99

said you had the important task of keeping the room from spinning. You were asleep before I even had a chance to say no."

Unsure if she was pulling my leg or not, I decided to let the matter lie.

When I was 18 or 19, I could go out to the bars in Montreal, hitting four or five of the best ones on Crescent Street on a typical Friday night. Back home for a couple of hours of sleep, and then it was back to the garage for a day's work. By nightfall I was ready for anything again.

By 1975, those days were over.

The rest of the morning was spent sitting around, letting the Aspirin, Rolaids and water do their work. Jen would come in to tease now and then, but it was all in good fun. Just before noon she cooked up a full course breakfast of bacon, eggs, hash browns and French toast.

The rest of the weekend was spent with our minds on things other than work. Tony Bakerstein, Mark Simson, Stubby Booker and the rest of the characters in my stories were far from my thoughts.

The sunny Sunday was spent driving the back roads and staring in awe at the leaves. Once we got lost, but didn't really care, eventually finding our way back to civilization. Even King enjoyed the ride, spending much of the time with his face in the wind, drinking in the smells of rotting leaves, cow pastures and freshly harvested corn fields.

On the way home we passed by Dunham, getting a glimpse of the family farm in its fall outfit. I was not disappointed, but did feel the familiar pang that struck me the last time I'd been there. Like it was mine, but didn't belong to me anymore. For an instant my mind flashed back to the man I'd seen on the tractor, and I missed farming, and the life that could have been.

"I'm going to have to find that woman from Brome Fair who knew my parents," I said to no one in particular, though Jen was the only one in the car, other than King.

"How are you going to do that, short of knocking on every door around here for miles?"

"Well, I figure that she came to the booth that day to renew her subscription. So if I can get a list from circulation of the people that renewed that day I should be able to see who signed up from this area. That should narrow things down a bit."

"Quite a bit, considering who reads the Granby Liar," she replied with a grin.

"It shouldn't be too hard," I said, ignoring her sarcasm.

***

Monday I was back in the saddle at work, though it felt more like the saddle was on me. The weekend had been far too short, made even shorter by the necessary hangover recovery time.

It was a quiet morning, and Rachel's weekend would be filling a lot of space, so I decided to start off by rewriting the piece on The Farm. I kept it relatively brief, about 12 inches in all. I used the "This wasn't supposed to happen" quote and a line or two from the grief-stricken girl. I made mention of their desire to create a perfect world, but didn't dwell on it. There was only so much you could say without making it sappy and maudlin.

From there I went on to look over the stacks of newspapers, paying particular attention to the Montreal Star and The Gazette. It would be nice to say that I was working hard, but I was actually killing time until something came up that I would have to do.

In reporters terms I had hit the wall. After the first few months at a new job it suddenly becomes hard to write. You avoid the keyboard and do whatever you can to write as little as possible. When you do write the words come out stilted, uneven, awkward.

After a week or two the feeling passes, only to return occasionally for the rest of your writing days. Sometimes it's easier to shake off, sometimes it's harder.

I then decided to delay a little longer by asking about the lady from Brome Fair. Not the one that beat me up, the other one. A trip to the circulation department was in order.

Wendy was a short brunette with a smooth-skinned round face and shocking big blue eyes. Though she wasn't your typical beach babe she had no problem getting dates. Word around the office was she had no trouble keeping them coming back for more.

I was surprised to see how protective she was of the subscribers' list. At first she said she didn't have time, and that she wasn't supposed to show the list to anyone.

"I just want some little old lady's name, that's all," I said, pleading. "It's not like I'm planning to rob her."

"What's in it for me?" she asked as she stretched her arms in front of her, bringing them together so that they pushed up her cleavage. Her eyes blue fire.

So this is why she has no problem getting dates.

"My eternal gratitude," I said, trying as hard as I could to maintain eye contact and still get a gawk at the cleavage. I was unable to think of anything I could offer that was appropriate.

A little more coaxing and she handed over the entire subscription list, some 4,000 names, which would have made my task a huge one indeed. A little more coaxing and she agreed to fish through her files from the list of renewals from Brome Fair.

Though Jen was being sarcastic when she made the comment about the small number of people who read the Granby Liar, her prediction about narrowing down the possibilities was on target. There was only one renewal from Dunham, one Alice Day.

I was scribbling down the address when Linda called out from the newsroom. Phone call.

"Is this Dave Rogers?" came the voice. It seemed familiar, but I couldn't place it.

"Yes."

"Tony crossed the wrong people."

"I figured that," I said as I tried to reach for a notepad that was nearly out of reach. "What can you tell me?"

"The guy is a bad cat. Tony and the guys had a deal with him, but Tony didn't like it. He decided one day when he was running across the border to take his bag to someone else, make more money. That didn't win him any favors with his employer."

"How do you know about all of this?" I asked.

"I can't really say. I know some things, that's all."

"Can I ask you your name."

"That's not a very good idea. Let's just call me Linus."

"Okay Linus. Did his employer have him killed?"

"He probably did the job himself. He's mean enough for that."

"Who is he?"

"I'd rather not say. This whole thing is really dangerous, and more people could get hurt. People who I really care about."

"Is there any way I can confirm this?"

"Not that I can think of. Look, I'm taking a big chance here, but I had to tell someone. A lot of good people could get hurt."

There was a pause as I tried to think of what to ask next. I could hear the faint sound of traffic in the background. Linus was probably at a pay phone.

"Were you one of the guys running the stuff across the border?" I asked.

"Look, I've got to go. I can't really say any more than I have."

"But-," I said before being met with the sound of a dial tone. Conversation over.

Damn, damn, damn.

I dropped the receiver back into the cradle and considered my options. I now had information that Tony Bakerstein had been working for some bad guy, smuggling dope across the border. He double crossed him and ended up dead for his trouble. Which was kind of what I already suspected.

However, I had no way of confirming the information and didn't know who I'd been talking to. I could use an unnamed source if I knew it was reliable, but I wasn't going to stake my reputation on an anonymous phone call. He could be full of shit, but I had a gut feeling he was serious. Linus made sure I couldn't use his information.

Damn, damn, damn.

Still charged up from the phone call, I decided to call Fernand Dubois to see if the cops had anything new. If they could tie Bakerstein to the drug smuggling ring then maybe I could use at least some of the information. But Dubois wasn't much help.

"Off the record, we are working with the hypothesis that he was involved with the smuggling. But we really don't know for sure, and we sure as hell can't say that on the record."

"There's no way we can get around this?" I asked, pushing.

"I'm not paid to compromise a police investigation so you can get a story. The investigation is continuing, that's all I can say."

Damn, damn, damn.

I went back to my story about the shocked people at the hippie commune. In the background 'graph about the earlier pot raid I added a sentence: "Police have not yet confirmed if the drug smuggling operation and the shooting of Bakerstein are connected."

I wasn't able to say it outright, but at least I could imply that the shooting and the drug smuggling were connected. Readers would get the idea, even though I didn't actually say so. It frustrated me that I had information I couldn't print. It frustrated me that I was at a dead end.

18

Life isn't like the movies, where the ace reporter can spend all of their time working on a single story, and nothing else matters. There's space to be filled and there isn't the time to devote all of your energy to one thing that may or may not produce a story right away, if ever. If there was, you wouldn't have much to read when you picked up your copy of whatever it is you read with your morning coffee.

In the movies the main character can think of nothing else, spurred on by a burning desire for the truth. In real life I went home Monday night, took the dog for a walk and spent a good chunk of the evening talking with Jen about the things our friends in the city were doing.

My life not being a movie, Tuesday my energies were not to be focused on The Farm and Tony Bakerstein. I had two press conferences in the morning. One was at the Granby Hospital, the announcement of the purchase of new heart monitors. The other was a bitch session held by the local Union Nationale riding association. Robert Bourassa and his Liberals were ruining the province with their policies, with Bill 22, and by just plain being Liberal. They predicted an easy victory for the Union Nationale when an election was called next year.

They never even considered the possibility that the Parti Québécois could win. Neither did a lot of people.

I was still running smack into the wall, so the stories were a little shorter than they might have been. I plowed on with the Underwood, banging out the words, one way or another. The prose was almost painful, and I imagined my readers would be able to spot every break in my stream of consciousness, every fragmented sentence. It's usually only felt by the writer, thankfully.

Wednesday John McAuslan, Rachel and Steve Farnham decided to go out for lunch, so I tagged along. I never went out for lunch, so it was a nice treat. A couple of beers to go with burgers at the Barrel was also a nice touch. By the time we returned to the office we were all feeling a little freer, like it was Friday. Anything is possible when you drink in the afternoon.

Sitting on my desk was a brown envelope. No address, no return address, no stamp. Someone had delivered it.

"Who's this from?" I asked Linda.

"Some guy came by while you were gone. I've never seen him before. Big guy, curly hair, like an afro."

I tore the end off of the envelope and pulled out the single sheet loose leaf of paper. Three words. Black marker.

ROGERS: BACK OFF!

I felt a quick twinge, like a serpent, course through my chest. What in hell was this?

I handed the letter to McAuslan.

"Shit man, seems you got some fan mail."

Rachel got up from her desk to see what was going on.

"Have you been pissing off someone we don't know about?"

"Back off from what?" I said. "I don't think I've been too hard on anyone in particular lately."

I was more puzzled than anything else. I could see getting hate mail if I'd run someone through the mill lately, but nothing came to mind. My stories on the shooting weren't pointing the finger at anyone in particular, and I hadn't really gone far beyond what the police were saying.

It wasn't hard to remember Jen's run-in at the library a couple of weeks ago. Same note, same big guy with curly hair. Same message.

But back off from what? The first note came after the raid on the commune, but before the discovery of the body. The hippies didn't seem like the type to go around threatening people. They probably didn't even read our paper.

When afro man passed the first note to Jen, I had figured it had something to do with the Mark Simson murder. But since then I hadn't even mentioned Simson's name.

The others didn't seem to be very concerned over the letter, and within a few minutes they were all back at their desks. Except for Steve Farnham, who was off to check out a high school football practice in Cowansville. The Massey-Vanier Vikings were looking particularly hard to beat this year, a collection of 200 pound plus farm boys.

I went through the motions that afternoon while my mind kept wandering back to the note. Last time I had it narrowed down to Stubby Booker because of the story that Bankroft had changed to make it look like he was responsible for Mark Simson's murder. But I hadn't even come close to mentioning his name in this story or any other lately.

Back off. Back off from what? Whoever it was seemed to want me to back off from at least two different stories. Stories which had no apparent relationship with each other. Murder of a cattle rustler in a prison. Murder of a hippie running drugs.

Could Stubby Booker be the bad guy they were doing the border runs for?

In one way it added up conveniently, but in another it didn't make sense. I'd heard that Stubby was into the cannabis trade, but what was he doing dealing with a bunch of hippie draft dodgers? He had his own people, and no shortage of other locals hoping to make a quick buck. Stubby didn't seem like the kind of guy to be hanging around with the peace and love set, people who could just as easily vanish over the border with his dope and never be seen again. At least the locals had to come home eventually.

***

Stubby Booker's place consisted of an immaculate two-storey house surrounded by a series of warehouses. During the day as many as ten men worked in and around the property, fixing farm machinery, warehousing construction materials, fixing cars. Cogs in Bookers well-oiled machine.

For the most part the men who worked the yard were kept in the dark when it came to the illegal activities. Trucks came and went, deals were made behind closed doors, and as few people knew about it as possible.

The chosen few who were in the know were sworn to secrecy, knowing full well that to speak to the wrong people would mean more than getting fired. More likely getting fired upon. They dealt with the much larger network that rarely set foot on Booker's property, keeping between them and the regular employees.

But when the provincial police, joined by the local RCMP detachment arrived at Roxton Pond Building Supply that Thursday morning, it was well before the hired help had arrived.

While nearly 20 police officers began milling around the yard a tall broad-shouldered detective pounded on the door of the clapboard house. Stubby lived alone, and the detective was more than a little surprised to see Booker show up at the door, his boots and coat already on. He didn't know that Booker rarely slept more than five hours a night, and was usually up by 5 a.m.

"Sanford Booker, we have reason to believe that there are stolen building materials on your property. We have a warrant to search your property," the detective said. He handed over a folded paper.

Booker smiled and stuffed the paper in his pocket without reading it. He knew they would have crossed all the t's and dotted the i's. His lawyer would worry about the technicalities later.

"You guys are gonna look like assholes when you come up empty," he said. "Again."

Booker then pushed past the tall man, walking into the yard. The detective nodded to two uniformed officers who went after him.

"Mr. Booker," one of them said nervously. "We have to take you in for questioning."

"And let you assholes root around here and plant whatever evidence you want? I don't think so boy."

"We have to take you in, sir," said the second uniform.

Stubby's neck began to turn red, the veins pushing their way to the surface. Everything Stubby does serves a purpose, and he knew there was no amount of screaming and threats that would make this situation go away. He would have to bide his time, extracting his revenge when the time was right.

"Fuck," he said through clenched teeth.

The detective was now lighting a Player's Navy Cut with a Zippo lighter. He was thinking of his early days on the force. A fellow patrol officer, young and cocky. Said he was going to change the world. He was going to get Stubby Booker, and then his reputation and career would be set.

Then he didn't show up for work one day. Didn't show up for work again ever, as a matter of fact.

This was the third time the detective was spearheading a raid on Booker's holdings. He hated the man, knowing full well that if there was a way out, Booker would find it. He knew well enough that until the judge's gavel pronounced sentence on this vile little man, anything could happen.

"Cuff him," the detective said, wanting to heap as much abuse on Booker as he could in the time he had before the dirty little man with the one eyebrow called his lawyer and walked away. He might not go to jail, but at least something would have been done. Something to honor a ghost from the past.

"And make sure he doesn't have anything on him," the detective added. "Pat him down."

A few minutes later, just as the two uniforms were leading Stubby Booker to the back seat of a waiting police cruiser, a man with a camera stepped out of a battered Buick LeSabre. He had just enough time to snap a single shot of Booker being tucked into the cruiser. One shot, but if the focus was right he knew it was front page stuff for the Granby Liar. And he knew the focus was right.

**

The morning Stubby Booker got busted Linda called John McAuslan. He made the phone calls, went to the arraignment and did all of the legwork on that one.

In the newsroom at the Granby Liar no one owned any given story or subject matter. Once again this wasn't the movies, where anything to do with a given subject is immediately handed to the star so he or she can work their magic.

Personally I was glad it wasn't me covering the raid. I was a little put off by the fan mail I'd gotten the day before, and Stubby seemed to be a possible sender. If it had been him and he saw me sitting there in the courtroom when he was charged, he'd probably get really mad. I didn't feel I needed that right now.

Thinking about things a little more, I realized that this would be a good test to see if Stubby was in any way connected to the ROGERS: BACK OFF note. After all, McAuslan had a golden opportunity to run Booker through the mud. If Booker didn't like his name in the paper, he'd be mad at McAuslan, not me. All I had to do was wait to see if McAuslan and I were on the same shit list or not.

McAuslan's story, written later that day, was one of those ones that made for good reading. An informant had made a deal with Booker for a truckload of stolen concrete mix. Money changed hands, allegedly between Booker himself and the informant, while the cops watched from a safe distance.

But when the cops went to Booker's, they couldn't find the stolen concrete. They couldn't even find the truck.

"A thorough search of the property turned up little, except for an unregistered handgun in Booker's house," the story said. "The long-barreled revolver has been confiscated by police, and Booker will most likely face firearms charges."

"The police will be lucky if even that charge manages to stick," McAuslan's story continued. "Booker has a long history of run-ins with the law, but Roxton Pond's most notorious businessman always manages to escape the clutches of law enforcement."

"There," I thought as I read McAuslan's story. "That points a finger better than anything I've done. He basically called him a career criminal."

As I sat back in my office chair that Friday morning, I figured McAuslan's story would certainly stir things up enough to answer my questions. If Booker wasn't mad at him, he sure as hell wouldn't be mad at me. Then, providing it wasn't Booker, I'd have to figure out who had been sending me the love notes.

There was one fly in the ointment, however. The front-page picture was strangely familiar. It looked like the dirty little guy with one eyebrow who gave me a hard time at the restaurant in Cowansville a few months earlier. But it was a profile shot and my restaurant encounter had been brief. After studying the photo for a few minutes I was no longer sure it was the same guy.

I was still going over the possibilities in my head when John McAuslan got back from Booker's bail hearing. Booker had spent Thursday night in jail, and apparently was in a foul mood. Foul, but still respectful of the judge.

"His lawyer is calling it an illegal search," McAuslan said. "He's also accusing the police of harassment, illegal surveillance and planting the handgun."

"So what is Booker facing?" I asked.

"For now they've got him on the handgun charge. They may still charge him with the stolen concrete, but they're waiting to find it first. No luck so far."

Booker was released on $500 bail and ordered to keep the peace. He was due to appear in court again in mid-November.

Later that day McAuslan checked in with Fernand Dubois to see if anything new had developed in the case. Dubois had little to add. They still hadn't found the cement mix. They were sending the pistol out for ballistics tests, but that would take at least two weeks, if not three. It seemed that Booker had little to fear from the law enforcement community.

19

Stubby Booker was back in Roxton Pond by lunchtime Friday. He drove his red GMC to John's Cantine for lunch. He sat alone, none of the regulars daring to ask about the raid, or the Granby Liar story.

After he left they all noted that Stubby was awfully quiet. With the exception of his face and neck turning a little red when he picked up the paper, he seemed remarkably composed. Though Booker had done and said nothing of note during his hour at the cantine, the regulars spent hours talking about it.

Later that afternoon Stubby was in his office when he got the call. Time for a meeting.

The following evening, with the sun setting off an explosion of fall colour, a freshly bathed and shaven Stubby Booker stepped out of his house and into his truck. Kicking up the blanket of fall leaves as he went, Booker headed south, bypassing Granby on Route 139. The road was only a few years old, and it was a hell of a lot faster than the old road, he thought.

Booker turned right onto Magenta Road, the pavement quickly giving away to gravel. When he got to the covered bridge he flicked on the headlights, the sun having mostly faded from view.

He turned right again into the driveway of a farm that seemed to be dying of neglect. The sway backed roofs casting sharp silhouettes against the little light that remained. There were no lights, no barking dogs. No one lived here. No one, not even Stubby's closest associates, knew he owned it. Property taxes were paid by a numbered company.

Booker guided the truck around behind the barn, slapping it into Park. He got out and walked up the barn bridge to open the doors.

Ten minutes later a midnight blue Cadillac Fleetwood pulled out of the yard with its lights off. Stubby, now wearing a tie to go with the rest of his suit, was at the wheel. A half-mile down the road he flicked the lights on and began the hour-long drive to Montreal.

After crossing the Champlain Bridge Booker took the Atwater exit, his car looking much like any other luxury car bearing people to the Forum for a night of hockey. The Detroit Red Wings were in town, and old rivalries promised a good game. A game Stubby had no intention of seeing.

A few blocks before the Forum Stubby turned left onto St-Jacques, and a few blocks later turned left again onto Walker Street. A third left took him into an alley behind a chocolate factory. He pulled his Cadillac into a space next to two others that were already there.

Wiping a thin layer of sweat from his brow, Booker took a set of welded steel stairs to a windowless door on the second floor with no outside handle. He knocked and was greeted by an olive-skinned man with large hands. Stubby was frisked, his snub-nosed .38 (a temporary replacement) was taken, and he was led into a windowless office. Booker was greeted by another deeply tanned man, dressed in an immaculate suit. He was smoking one of those green cigars that come in an aluminum tube.

"So what in hell is going on out there in the Wild West?" the man said bluntly after the niceties had been exchanged. "Seems there's a lot more action out there than I'd like to see."

"We've had a few problems. Nothing that can't be ironed out," Stubby said in a respectful tone.

"But now you've gotten yourself arrested. We don't like dealing with people who attract attention, and you seem to be doing just that lately."

"That's nothing. Some little prick decided to burn me on a load of concrete. The cops can't see any further than that, and they have no reason to."

The man stood up and walked around the desk, sitting on the front edge. He stared for a few seconds at the tip of the cigar, then turned his gaze down on Booker.

"Look. I don't give a damn what you do out there in the sticks. You can proclaim yourself king if you want. But some very important people are waiting for payment."

"There's been a few..."

"I'm not done yet, so don't interrupt me," the man said as he stared once again at the tip of the cigar. "In case you haven't been keeping up with things that aren't happening in your little kingdom, there's a lot of shit going on in the real world. Most of it requires money or guns. We gave you your guns, but I'm still waiting for my money."

"I had to change gears after the Vermont State Troopers got my runners. Things will be up to speed very soon, trust me," said Stubby, the tone always respectful. "I got rid of the draft dodgers and got some good local people. More dependable. I'll have more money coming in within a week or so."

"When do I get my $100,000?" the man said into his cigar.

"Soon. Two weeks, tops."

"I know some people who like to make loans, but I've always found it to be nothing but trouble. That's why I accepted to do business with you in the first place. It was all cash, no bullshit for years. Now it seems you're having a tough time keeping up."

The fact of the matter was that Stubby could come up with the money if he dug into his other operations. But he wanted the gun money to come from the smuggling, leaving everything else for himself. Making the mob wait for payment also gave Stubby a feeling of control that he liked. He liked it a lot.

He also liked the idea of getting pacifist peace-loving hippies to smuggle pot across the line so he could make money to buy guns. Guns intended to stave off the separatists and maybe start a small war if need be.

"I'll have all of your money in ten days," Stubby replied, rising to the challenge from the olive-skinned cigar smoker.

"Done."

The cigar smoker visibly relaxed, apparently pleased with the results of the meeting. His next question caught Stubby completely off guard.

"This little group of yours. What are they supposed to do, start a revolution or something?"

Booker's face paled slightly. He had never mentioned anything about the group to anyone in the Montreal mafia. But they always seemed to know what was going on, even out in the country. Making a mental note to himself to tighten up security a few more notches, he decided to act as if it was all common knowledge.

"A lot of things are changing, and a lot of us are nervous. René Levesque and the Parti Québécois stand a chance in the next election, and the English people of this province will have to defend themselves. The FLQ made us all into victims five years ago. We don't want to feel that way ever again."

"And if you make a few dollars in the process, so much the better?" the olive-skinned cigar smoker asked.

Stubby said nothing, allowing only the faint traces of a smile to cross his face.

***

The People for an English-Speaking Quebec, or PESQ, started as a loose association of Townshippers from a variety of backgrounds who mainly shared a fear of all things French. Some were ex-military types, frustrated that they never got to be in real combat and hoping to stir something up. Others were factory workers and farmers increasingly worried about the separatists and the Front de Libération du Québec, the terrorist group which had captured the headlines with mailbox bombings and the October Crisis of 1970.

By 1975 the main FLQ terrorists had been arrested or exiled, but a lot of Quebecers, French and English alike, were afraid there were still others out there. With the nationalist movement on the rise, some people were increasingly concerned that it could all turn into a bloody revolution.

In 1974 PESQ was formed by a half-dozen people who could no longer control their paranoia sitting around a kitchen table in East Farnham. One was a former reservist with the Canadian Army. Soon after the first meeting he approached Ainsley Wright, a retired colonel, and the paramilitary group PESQ was born.

The formation of a military group didn't suit four of the founders. They were concerned, but didn't like the direction the group was taking. They walked away, agreeing to say nothing. Sensing the opportunity to put his leadership skills to the test once again, Colonel Wright set about making the group into a capable fighting force, able to react when the revolution came. As far as he was concerned, it was coming, and it would be his duty as a Canadian to put a stop to it.

If there was one thing the Colonel did right, it was maintaining secrecy. By the fall of 1975 he had over 100 foot soldiers in training, all with varying degrees of proficiency with firearms and explosives. The group trained regularly, but as yet police and government types had no idea of its existence. Even the local English population was largely unaware of the secret army, with each member sworn to absolute secrecy. In an area where rumors traveled faster than facts, PESQ wasn't even so much as a whisper in the night between lovers.

A large part of the secrecy was due to the fanatical loyalty of Wright's disciples. While the appropriateness of his actions might have been questionable to the rest of the world, no one in PESQ would have ever questioned Ainsley Wright's place as leader. His hold on his followers was unmistakable.

But while the militant group had a growing roster of willing local boys, it lacked the firepower that Ainsley Wright figured it deserved. He couldn't abide the thought of "his" men fighting with shotguns and deer rifles, but PESQ lacked both money and access to the real weapons of war. Wright even found himself contemplating burglarizing the military base in Farnham. He dismissed the idea, unable to commit a crime against an institution that he saw as a fundamental element of society.

In desperation and amid a growing sense of fear that the revolution might happen before PESQ could get ready, Wright decided to make a deal with the devil.

After a couple of meetings at Booker's house, the basics of the arrangement were made. Booker would provide the military hardware; assault rifles, grenade launchers and a selection of explosives. In exchange he would be named the second in command of PESQ. Second in command, but most of his newfound underlings still didn't know he was involved. He was to remain, for all intents and purposes, a silent partner.

On the surface it seemed like a boon for the militia group, and once the deal was sealed Wright thought he'd scored a major coup. He was still the leader, and a large part of the success of the group would depend on his well-honed ability to plan and act when the blood would begin spilling into the streets.

Col. Wright apparently had no idea who he was dealing with.

Booker had other things in mind. He was happy to have the Colonel running things while he watched from the sidelines, biding his time. After all, there was the very slight possibility of a revolution, though Booker doubted it. If it did happen it could be useful to have a seasoned military man and a standing army ready. If a time came when it looked like nothing was going to come of Quebec's warming political climate, then Booker figured he'd find a way to turn the group to serve his purposes. Not too many people have their own standing army after all. He hadn't decided what purpose it would serve, but there was still time to think about the possibilities...

Using the hippies to make the gun money meant Stubby held his position of power without the usual financial risk. In other words, for no cost he was now a heartbeat away from being able to inflict a lot of damage on anyone or anything he wanted. Then not even the Montreal mafia would be able to touch him without making things messy. That was the dream.

Fall provided an excellent cover for training, with a lot of the members already being avid hunters. As far as their friends, wives and children were concerned, they were just heading off to shoot a few partridges, or maybe a deer. Before and after hunting season alibis were covered with fishing expeditions or a trip to the woods for target practice.

Sometimes hunting was used as training, allowing the men to bring home some game. But the occasional deer that was shot was brought down with several full metal jacket rounds from a Belgian-made military issue FN, not from the lever action Winchester that typically hung on the rack in the kitchen.

About 15 miles southeast of Cowansville, on the other side of Knowlton, lay a gigantic property owned by Dominion Pulp and Paper. The company owned 10,000 acres in the Sutton Mountains, from which they harvested pulpwood for their mills. The bulk of the property was in a bowl, surrounded by mountain peaks and therefore insulated from the outside world. The sharp sounds of rifle practice or explosives training was never heard outside of the bowl.

Getting to the property meant taking a number of back roads that got narrower as they wound their way up into the mountains. Once on the property the PESQ freedom fighters could make use of the dozens of roadways and trails that had been left behind by the logging crews and their equipment.

The size of the property gave PESQ a degree of security that couldn't be found elsewhere. The pulp loggers could only work a small part of the property at any one time, rarely venturing beyond the 200 or 300 acre section they'd clear out in a season. That left PESQ with 9,700 acres to train in.

To further tighten security, Wright made sure the men typically trained in groups of ten, with each group in a different area. If caught they could pass themselves off as hunters or poachers, and the secrecy of the group could be maintained. Except for the cell leaders, the men had no idea who was outside their own cell.

At the end of every training session the men were under strict orders to go straight home. No stopping at a bar for a beer, on threat of immediate dismissal from PESQ. For the followers, that was threat enough, and no one had dared break the code so far.

But despite the fanatical attention to secrecy, the Montreal mob knew about PESQ.

Shortly after midnight that starlit October Saturday Stubby Booker raced his Cadillac along the Eastern Townships Autoroute, barely pausing to toss a quarter at the tollbooths. On the radio the overnight news reader was droning on about the Red Wings victory, but Booker didn't even notice.

Stubby's main thoughts were on how his Montreal associates had learned about PESQ. How much did they know? Who else could possibly know?

There was a leak somewhere, and as soon as Stubby found out where he was going to plug it. With lead if he could get away with it.

20

I woke early Saturday morning, thanks mainly to King, who was scratching at the door to go out. The 7 a.m. morning sun was bright and clear, but not yet strong enough to melt the heavy layer of frost that stiffened the lawn. The large X design on the hood of the Falcon was etched in a thin layer of ice particles.

As I've said before, I'm not a morning person. My being awake early enough to see the frost was stranger still because my thoughts had been keeping me awake the night before.

Mostly my thoughts had been about my family, and the holes both in the memories I had and in the stories I'd been fed by the few relatives I knew. I had the basics on who my forefathers were and what they did, but my father's story was never given with such ease. What few words I could coax from my mother were halting, heavily edited. Most of my relations had died off, taking their memories with them. Typical Rogers fashion: stubborn, stoic, closed mouthed bunch. Even as one of them I often had no idea what they were really thinking.

For many years those few scant words and the select scenes that flashed in my memories were enough to sustain my curiosity and keep my father's memory alive. But my return to the Eastern Townships and the old Rogers family stomping grounds was slowly forcing me to search for more. Like a pebble in a shoe, it nagged me.

My best bet for finding the missing information appeared to be Alice Day, the nice lady I'd met at Brome Fair, not long before Mark Simson's mom tried to show me her appreciation of my work.

While waiting for the kettle to boil I took out the scrap of paper with her name, address and phone number on it. A twinge of both excitement and fear ran through my body, excitement at the possibility of learning what I needed to know, and fear at the possibilities I might find.

I brought two steaming mugs of coffee to the bedroom, pausing briefly to look at my beautiful sleeping wife. I have always believed the benchmark of a woman's beauty is in how they looked in the morning, before the showers, hair and makeup. As I placed the coffee on the end table I was comforted by the sight of her slender beauty. Beauty that for some reason, had chosen to love me.

Men are buffoons. It always amazes me that women would have any interest in us at all. We're generally a pretty clueless lot, prone to bad smells and poor life choices. But at a certain point you just have to stop wondering why, and accept their love for the blessing that it is.

As I sat on the edge of the bed she stirred, stretching her arms and legs, and growling ever so softly. The smell of the coffee opened her eyes slightly.

"What's up with you my faithful coffee man?" she asked.

"Couldn't sleep after King woke me up. Damn dog," I replied.

"I'm glad someone can get your lazy ass out of bed, 'cause God knows I can't."

"You probably won't pee on the carpet if I ignore you," I said.

"Oh, I don't know…"

We chatted and sipped our coffee, wide awake early on a day off. Meanwhile King had happily gone back to sleep on the couch in the living room.

"I think I'm going to call and see if I can talk to this Alice Day woman I told you about," I said. "I might be able to hear some neat stories from him about my dad."

"You'd better wait awhile to be sure she's up and around. Let's have an old-fashioned bacon and eggs breakfast first."

Mrs. Day was probably like most old ladies, up at the first hint of sunlight. Still, a good breakfast didn't sound like a bad idea, and it helped me to put off the phone call awhile longer.

By 9 a.m., the smell of bacon still in the air, I had the receiver in my one hand and Alice Day's phone number in the other. It took a few minutes to actually start dialing. She answered on the third ring.

"Mrs. Day, this is Dave Rogers from the Granby Leader-Mail. I believe we spoke at Brome Fair."

"Oh, yes, you were the one that got attacked by that woman with the jug," she said. "I do hope you're okay."

"Yes, I'm fine, thanks. Though it did slow me down for a few days."

"You Rogers boys are a tough lot," she said. "Takes more than a water jug to slow you down, I imagine."

I could hear a faint but strange sound, and immediately remembered her nervous habit of keeping her mouth in constant motion, talking or not. The image of her darting tongue entered my mind.

At first Mrs. Day was a little hesitant to talk to me about my family, but after a little prodding she agreed to let us drop by after lunch.

The tires of the Falcon crunched over a fresh layer of graded gravel as I turned off of Maska Road and onto Meigs. I would have missed the house entirely if it hadn't been for the silver mailbox with DAY painted boldly on it in red.

Alice Day lived alone in a neatly kept house that was little more than a cottage, surrounded on all sides by the neighbour's apple orchard. The house had probably originally served as quarters for the pickers that migrated to the region late every August, only to move on in October.

The heavy-set woman greeted Jen and I at the door, obviously pleased to have some company. There was a faint tint of blue in her hair, and a warm smile that appeared briefly when her mouth would stop moving.

We settled around the kitchen table, where we were greeted by Toby and Tyler, the two calico cats that she shared the house with. Chester, a huge mongrel of a dog that served as household protector, was barricaded in the back porch. After loudly letting it be known he was there, Chester settled down, occasionally taking deep sniffs from the bottom crack of the door.

"Just give me a moment to put some coffee on," Alice said, moving her large frame around the small kitchen with the ease of someone well accustomed to her space. No searching for utensils, no wasted effort. Like a short order cook working in one of those old streetcars converted into a restaurant.

"So you want to know more about your father," she said as she placed a plate of cookies on the table. "I really don't know where to begin."

"Well ma'am, he died when I was ten, so there isn't much I know about him. My mother told me a few things, but she doesn't like to talk about the past very much."

"Talking about the past is no problem for me," she replied. "I've got one heck of a lot of past behind me. It's the future I don't like to talk about."

As the coffee began to perk on the stove Alice Day began her narrative, which took little prompting. It was evident that she had told a tale or two in her time.

"When I first started working at your grandfather's, your father was probably about 12 years old. He was an active kid, always into something. If I remember right, the other kids called him Slippers, because he was always slipping in and out of places he wasn't supposed to be. Sometimes that meant slipping into places the other kids wouldn't dare to go. Like the belfry at the Anglican Church, or the roof of the Patterson's silo. He'd go places grownups wouldn't dare to go. They'd just have to sit and watch until he decided it was time to come down and get his punishment."

"One Halloween your father got together with three or four other boys in Dunham. They held the ladder while he climbed, taking people's laundry and stringing it up on the electrical wires. The ladder wasn't leaning against anything, you see. The boys held the bottom as best they could, and your father would balance his way to the top, laundry in hand. He was always sure on his feet."

"Sounds like a bit of a daredevil," I said

"Lands sakes yes," she said. "I'm sure your grandmother didn't live as long as she could have, worrying about Davie like she did. "But he never seemed to notice."

"As he got older he gained a reputation for being a bit of a wild one. The type that mothers try to keep their daughters away from. It wasn't just the high places anymore. Davie liked to have fun, and he'd go just about anywhere to find it. Sometimes he found trouble as well."

"When we met at the fair you said he was 'almost notorious,' is that what you meant?" I asked.

She was quiet for a moment, staring at her coffee cup. Choosing her words.

"He started to calm down when he met your mother. A good woman she was. Took good care of your grandmother. How's your mom doing anyways?"

It took a few minutes to steer the conversation back to my dad. She was a skilled conversationalist, and it was hard to nail her down. I finally went for the direct approach.

Another pause. The cuckoo clock by the cellar door seemed unusually loud. I decided to let the silence ask the question.

"By the time you came along he seemed to be settling down, though I don't think it was easy for him. He loved the farm like he loved your mother. I think everyone was shocked when he moved away. And so suddenly, too."

"Why did we move?" A question that I'd asked my mother numerous times over the years and had never been happy with the response.

Yet another pause. In her eyes I could see a decision being made. Then the expression on her faced relaxed a bit.

"We don't know for sure. The rumour was that he was in some kind of trouble. But to tell the truth from what I saw his trouble days were becoming a thing of the past. Still, people like to talk, whether they know what they're talking about or not."

"Are you saying he was running away from something?" Jen asked. "What could he have been into?"

"Well, you have to remember that your grandfather was into the moonshine business, and I think your father was too. For a little while. Of course we might just be tarring him with the same brush. Personally I never saw anything that would have given you're father the reputation he had. He liked to have fun, but he didn't drink any more than anyone else, and in those days drugs were what we'd heard people in the city did."

Jen and I continued asking questions, but Mrs. Day wouldn't be nailed down. I decided to ease off. After all this was an old lady who knew my parents nearly 30 years ago, not some criminal having to sweat it out under a bright light.

Far from answering my questions, the visit to Mrs. Day left me scratching my head for the rest of the afternoon and into the evening. All I had really learned was that my dad had a bit of a reputation, possibly because there were moonshiners in the family, or possibly because he liked to live a little closer to the edge than those around him. Not much to go on.

***

In my dream I am standing on the top of a silo. I immediately drop to my stomach, clutching for the lightning rod. How in hell did I get up here? Why is it so damned windy?

My dad's face appears over the edge of the curved roof. Like a cat he jumps from the top rung of the ladder to the roof next to me. He's as comfortable as if he's standing in our living room.

"What are you doing?" I shriek. Not even a chance of acting calm in this situation. I'm panicking. He thinks it's funny.

"This, this is nothing," he says through a wide grin. "I've climbed to higher places than this. No different than being at ground level, just a better view that's all."

"But how did I get up here?"

"Probably got curious. That's how it all starts. You wonder what it's like. Sooner or later you go try to find out for yourself. Sound familiar?"

"What do you mean?"

"You got curious. Now you're putting yourself in a situation where it's not so much fun anymore. Or maybe it is fun. You having fun?"

"No, I want to get down."

"There's an easy way down. Just a step or two."

He starts to dance a jig. I remember that jig from when I was a kid. He used to do it in the kitchen when he was joking around with mother. Kind of Irish, mostly made up. All dad.

It panics me even further.

"Stop it, you're not in the kitchen dad!"

"It's just like the kitchen, except for this curved bit here. It's all like it's supposed to be, son. This is who I am. You've just never seen this part of me."

"I've seen enough, thanks. Please stop."

"Don't worry. You'll never see everything. I mean, who sees everything? Who would want to?"

"I just want to know who you are. Or were."

"You'll never know it all. Not even your mother knows it all. Hell, I don't think I even know it all. People are like that. More colours than fall a life has. More colours than you'll ever see."

"But I miss you. I miss you and I barely know who it is I'm missing."

"Well when I try to give you advice you ignore me. Sure know where you got that hard head of yours from."

"Dad, can you get me down from here?"

"What's the matter? Scared little boy? Got himself someplace he doesn't want to be? Just climb down, that's all."

To make his point he starts dancing again, ever close to the curved edge of the silo roof. God we're high up. As if sensing my growing panic he dances faster, closer to the edge.

"Dad, no!"

And then he slips. He holds onto the cable for the lightning rod for a few seconds, and for the first time I see fear in his face. He's scared. Scared of more than falling. An instant later he's gone.

I am alone, clinging to the lightning rod. No one will rescue me. No one will ever really understand. No one will ever really know.

I wake up in my bed, Jen sleeping next to me. Overcome by a feeling of loneliness that makes my eyes water and won't let go.

21

Raoul Castonguay lived on a small farm at the end of Lawrence Road in Brigham. It was quiet, out of the way, and totally impossible to make a living off of. But that didn't matter much, because Castonguay's survival depended more on his work within the separatist Parti Québécois than it did on his country hideaway.

Castonguay was a party bagman, raising money for the PQ by networking with special interest groups, businesspeople and those wealthier party members who believed the only answer to Quebec's problems lay in cutting its ties with the rest of Canada and going it alone. Allegations that he had ties with radical separatist groups like the FLQ had never been proven. Publicly he carried an air of refinement, wrapping his portly build in tailored suits and surrounding himself with Quebec's beautiful people.

Castonguay was good at his job, and in October 1975 he had been doing particularly well, building up the party's coffers for the next election campaign. A campaign he believed the PQ could win, even if many of the leading pundits had written the separatists off as a fringe group.

But when the time came to rest and recharge his batteries, Castonguay left his posh Montreal apartment and expensive tailored suits for his scrubby little farm in the Townships with the well-maintained Victorian style house.

Not many locals knew that Castonguay had a home in the region. But someone at the People for an English-Speaking Quebec found out about it, and his farm was targeted for PESQ's first public act.

Ainsley Wright had been hesitant at first, stating that he was more comfortable with continuing to train secretly in case separatist fervor got out of hand. But the feeling among his followers was that the frogs should know what they would have to deal with if they tried to split up the country.

In the end a compromise was reached. PESQ members would slip in late at night, set Castonguay's aged barn on fire, and slip away. That way it was unlikely anyone would be harmed, but a message would be sent. A carefully crafted note would make the message clear, but would have no fingerprints. It would make PESQ's existence known for the first time.

Stubby Booker wasn't there with the rest of the leadership for the debates on moving from a state of readiness to small scale acts of terrorism. But Ainsley Wright, true to the deal he made, kept Booker informed. Booker let it be known that he favored a trial run. He wanted to see what his fledgling private army could do.

The barn fire bothered Wright, the act running up against his law and order values. But he comforted himself with the thought that there were worse things than burning an empty barn. It was an act that would only really affect a traitor, he consoled himself.

Just before midnight on the third Saturday in October four men in army surplus battle fatigues shivered in the back of a Ford F-100 as it turned off of des Érables onto Lawrence Road. Two others, dressed more like hunters than guerilla soldiers, sat in the cab. As the truck approached a farm where the road takes a sharp left the driver flicked off the headlights.

The truck slowed enough to allow the four men to jump off, gear in hand, just like they'd practiced. Two stalkier men each carried five gallon gas cans. The other two, both taller and more finely built, carried two molotov cocktails each.

As the truck slowly made its way to the end of the road to turn around, the four made their way silently to the barn. Even Castonguay's dog, which slept on the screened in porch, failed to notice their arrival.

Like any empty barn in the Townships in 1975, Castonguay's wasn't locked. The foursome slipped in with little more than the grating of the rusty hinges, and within seconds were splashing gas around with abandon, driven by the thrill of the moment.

"We're making history man," said one of the stocky men, a little too loudly.

"Shut up," came the whispered reply, as if the hushed words in the barn would be enough to arouse Castonguay from his deep sleep 75 yards away. Or rouse the dog they'd seen when doing an earlier reconnaissance of the farm. It seemed to spend its nights in the house, or on the porch.

With the strong smell of gas following them the four men left the barn. While the heavier men began to make their way back to the road, the other two pulled out their glass bottles of gas, shaking them upside down to dampen the rags so they'd be easier to light.

The first two were thrown at the same time, making an audible Whoomp! The third missed the doorway, hitting the casing and spreading liquid fire up the side of the grey clapboards. Awake now Castonguay's dog could see the silhouette's of the two torch men against the flames, and began barking frantically.

"We gotta go, now!" said the one who missed the doorway. He turned and began heading for the roadway without another word.

The last man stared at the flames for a few seconds, a smile appearing from under the handlebar moustache. Calmly he turned towards the house, a molotov cocktail in one hand and a Zippo lighter in the other. He lit the rag, paused for a few seconds to make sure it was well lit, and then casually threw it onto the porch of the house.

"What the fuck are you doing, man?" came a frantic call from his partner, who was now well up the driveway.

"Special request."

"We weren't supposed to burn his house, for fuck's sakes!"

"You do your job. I'm doing mine."

With the dog's territorial barks of anger turning to yelps of fear, the man turned and began following his partner up the driveway, black leather combat boots crunching hard on the gravel.

Raoul Castonguay never saw any of the four men who set his barn and house on fire. He later told police he heard a vehicle, probably a truck, speeding away. He was too busy trying to save his black Labrador from his burning home.

Choking on smoke Raoul managed to get the dog out of the house. His companion, a younger man named Stéphane, just had time to phone for help before climbing out a rear window. Brigham didn't have a fire department, but nearby Adamsville did have a brigade of volunteers.

When the firefighters arrived about 15 minutes later Raoul, Stéphane and the black lab were standing in the barnyard, watching the spectacle in stunned silence. Castonguay was still breathing hard from the attempts to save what he could. The few belongings he had salvaged were strewn across the lawn in the back yard, heaved out through the windows as the smoke thickened around him.

The dozen or so firefighters weren't badly trained, and their equipment was fairly modern. But when a century-old clapboard house catches fire, it's hard to stop it. The firemen couldn't get inside, and the water supply was limited to a small pond about a dozen feet across and a shallow well. Their efforts soon focused on containing the fire and preventing its spread to the nearby forest, while tanker trucks set off in search of more water.

It would be another six hours before anyone noticed the note in the mail box.

***

I love chasing after a story as much as any other reporter. Still, when the phone rang at 1 a.m., I was less than pleased.

"Rogers, there's a fire out in your neck of the woods," Bankroft said before I was awake enough to respond. "Lawrence Road."

"Where did you get this from?" I asked, hoping for a way to stay in bed for the rest of the night.

"One of our freelance shooters, shit, what's his name, fat little bugger, aw damn. Anyways, he couldn't sleep so he was listening to his police scanner when he heard the call come in." Bankroft said. "Go check it out. He's on his way already."

Ten minutes later, my head still full of cobwebs, I made my way to the Falcon. Knowing I'd be there for awhile I put on a ski jacket Jen had dug out from the boxes a couple of days ago. I scraped the frost off the windshield while the motor warmed up. As I got in one of the valves finally stopped its rhythmic ticking.

Still wishing I was in bed, I found myself hoping the fire would be out by the time I got there. Then I would at least be able to nail a few quick and easy interviews and take off. But by the time I got out of Brigham heading for the Lawrence Road turnoff, I knew that wasn't the way my night would play out.

For one thing, I could smell the smoke from over a mile away. Heavy forest obscured the view, but I could see a reddish glow against the night sky.

I parked the Falcon on the side of the road, just past the farm so it wouldn't be in the way for the fire trucks. There were at least another dozen cars there, most of them belonging to firefighters, I figured.

Notepad in hand I walked down the gravel driveway, watching the scene unfold before me.

At centre stage the flames were licking into the sky, well above the roof. To the left a second building had already collapsed into a burning heap of rubble. A lone firefighter with a hose was working on the barn, while everyone else was focused on the house. Though I hadn't covered that many fires, I knew this house was a goner.

Standing off to one side were two men, one about 50 and the other seemingly a bit younger. They wore the calm, dignified expressions of those who are experiencing deep tragedy, but don't yet know how to react. A black dog on a leash sat on the left side of the older man, wearing a similar shocked expression.

Not yet ready to talk to those who I figured were the victims, I quietly made my way around behind the two, standing for a few minutes and continuing my observation of the scene. I pulled out my notepad, counting fire trucks and firefighters, noting the absence of an ambulance, and the presence of three police cruisers, their flashers strobing the surrounding fields.

One by one the fire hoses sputtered dry. In the lights of a pickup truck off to the right of the farmhouse it was easy to see that what had once been a small pond was now little more than a mud hole. Several firefighters could be heard yelling into hand held radios. A few moments of confusion later a firefighter with a long iron bar was forcing the concrete lid off the shallow well.

"Ce n'est pas assez," I heard the older man say in a low tone. It's not enough.

"Dans deux minutes ça va être le même problème, pas d'eau," the younger man said in a voice that was softer, almost a whisper. It will be the same problem in two minutes, no water.

About 15 minutes later I'd listed all of the interesting observations I could, leaving me with little else to do at the scene except interview the victim. I stalled for a few minutes more before approaching the man.

Raoul Castonguay spoke to me in the same shocked, almost hushed tone I'd' overheard already. His French was clean and educated, a reflection of his upbringing and education.

"Any idea who did this," I asked in French.

"Maybe it was you English people," he said with a smile that appeared for a brief instant before the shocked expression returned. Evidently he'd picked up on my accent.

"What do you do for a living?" I continued.

"I work for the Parti Québécois and the independence of Quebec," came the reply.

Politics between the English and French in Quebec is a dicey subject, one the two groups usually avoid in each other's presence. He said little more and I steered the conversation back to the fire, making a note to do some digging into Castonguay's background at the office Monday morning.

With little more to do I left the remains of Castonguay's retreat before the flames were out. There was little more to be done there, except shiver in the cold of an October night.

Late Sunday morning I took a drive by for a final look. Castonguay was gone, the only people there were a couple of crime scene investigators and an RCMP officer of some sort milling around in the smouldering rubble. Though it was rare to see a Mountie in the area, I didn't give it much thought.

Monday morning I was at my desk at the Granby Liar by 9 a.m., an unusually early start for a reporter. I spent about 20 minutes clearing off my desk and looking for ways to put off working. Then I gathered a stack of old newspapers and began looking for stories about the PQ, hoping to find something relevant.

I struck gold in a September issue of *La Presse,* realizing almost immediately that Castonguay's joke might not be that far off the mark.

The feature story outlined Castonguay's long held ties to the separatist movement, including the allegations of ties to the terrorist FLQ. In recent years his efforts had been focused on raising millions for the fledgling PQ. He was a close personal friend of party leader René Levesque, and true to his backroom reputation, was believed to have developed a number of the party's policies.

No mention of his home in the Townships. No one in the office seemed to know he lived here either.

The report on the 11 o'clock news from the local radio station made Castonguay's comments to me all that much more prophetic. A note had been found after the fire, with a group calling itself People for an English-Speaking Quebec claiming responsibility. I had Fernand Dubois on the phone before they'd moved on to the weather.

"What's this about the note?" I asked.

"One of the firefighters found it in the mail box Sunday morning," Dubois said.

Dubois wouldn't give out the text of the note, choosing instead to paraphrase it: PESQ, as he called it, said this was to serve as a warning to anyone who tried to break up the country, or make French the only language in Quebec.

"Off the record for a moment," Dubois said. "There were numbers and codes on the note. This is usually done so in the future we know it was them and not a copycat. These guys are planning to be around for awhile."

"On the record, have you ever heard of these guys before?" I asked.

"As far as we know this is the first time they've done anything in this area," he said. "We don't know much about them, but our investigation is continuing."

"Why was there an RCMP at the scene Sunday?" I asked.

"They always check into things when it's something political," Dubois said.

So what had started as a routine house fire that I had wanted to get out of, had turned into a story about a brand-new group of terrorists setting the house of a prominent separatist on fire. From where I sat, things were looking up.

I tried to get in touch with Castonguay again, but no luck. His phone in Brigham was somewhere at the bottom of a heap of rubble, and the number I managed to find in our only Montreal phone book (three years old), was out of service.

Rachel gave me the name of a local PQ organizer named Hubert Perron. When I asked him about the note he gave me a good earful of PQ political philosophy, followed by a speech on how the party would not be deterred in its efforts in achieving Quebec nationhood. He gave good quotes, but it was hard to sit there and listen to him rant about how the English would have to learn their place.

They were good quotes, but they wouldn't garner much sympathy for Castonguay's personal tragedy. No matter how I arranged them it looked like PESQ, whatever it was, had done the English community a service by burning this man out of his home. Sometimes a story comes out with its own slant, whether you like it or not.

22

The response to the story and the media frenzy it was brewing was nothing short of electric. French speakers suddenly became afraid of their English neighbors, while the English reactions ranged from support for PESQ to groans of disgust and talk of packing up and getting out of this political backwater. Though points of view varied, everyone seemed to be talking about it. Even the Montreal Star, which usually ignored anything off the island, had picked up on the Castonguay fire in its Tuesday edition.

On the way to work I stopped at John's Cantine for a coffee to go. I parked next to a red pickup and walked in on the middle of an animated conversation among the locals.

"Couldn't a happened to a nicer fella," one old man was saying. "Too bad he got out."

"They said in the Granby Liar he got all the hair burned off his arms," said a wood cutter in his 20's. I never wrote that, but decided not to correct him.

"How do you burn hair off a frog anyways," chimed in a short, dirty man sitting at the counter. The only one who seemed to notice me, he looked at me through narrowed eyes that peered out from under heavy, dark eyebrows and a yellow Caterpillar baseball hat.

"Who knows what to believe," he went on, still looking in my direction. "Fucking paper lies all the time anyways."

"Especially about you," the wood cutter said. A few of them laughed, but the dirty man did not.

It took me a few seconds before I realized the dirty man was Stubby Booker. He looked a little different from the picture we ran when he was arrested, but it was him just the same. I also realized he was the one I who'd given me a hard time at the restaurant in Cowansville not long after I started at the paper. The urge to get to work early became a little stronger.

I turned my back on the conversation when the coffee arrived, heading for the door. It wasn't the place for me to be preaching the virtues of the Granby Leader-Mail, especially with Booker in the room.

By the time I arrived at the office a note from Bankroft told me a follow up story on the Castonguay fire was needed, something I'd already figured out. I had planned to check on how things were going with the Tony Bakerstein murder investigation, but that would have to wait.

The big question was where to begin. I started by looking through the other papers to see what had been done elsewhere. The Star story took up a column on the front page and nearly half of A-2. La Presse relegated the story to Page 3, while the Journal de Montreal ran a fire photo and head shot on front, with a half page story on Page 12, followed by a sidebar on Page 13 outlining Castonguay's political career. True to its form, the Journal painted the story with a different brush, pointing to Castonguay's tireless efforts to make life better for the Quebec people.

There were a couple of things I noted in the other articles but nothing to really merit the follow-up my readers and now my boss were demanding. Fernand Dubois wouldn't have much to say this early in the morning either.

A call to the Granby RCMP detachment was met with the response that the fire was a provincial police matter, and they weren't involved in the investigation. The constable on the other end of the phone, whoever he was, wouldn't say why one of his own was at the fire scene Sunday.

As often happens when chasing a story, I didn't have much to go on. At least not this early in the morning.

***

Stubby Booker couldn't help but smile. PESQ's debut had been more impressive than he had hoped, helped along by the guy who decided it would be more effective to burn Castonguay's house than his barn.

On that count Ainsley Wright was furious. Never fully in favour of the move, he allowed the operation to go ahead with strict orders that no lives would be put in danger, and no serious damage be done. He was even more furious when he met with Booker at his house on Sunday, and Booker didn't seem to mind the fact that Castonguay's house had been torched.

"We aren't here to be terrorists," Wright had said. "We're only supposed to be here to keep them in their place."

"I think we sent the right message, maybe they'll think twice when they start going on about separation being peaceful," Booker replied. "Besides, Castonguay's a separatist bastard. Should've been hung for treason."

"That's not the way we do things," Wright said. "This is my outfit and we do things my way."

"You just remember who's footing the bill for this," Booker replied in a tone that was as even and quiet as Wright's was angry and loud. "I don't think it's a big deal."

"Well, that guy's out. Finished."

"No he's not. You leave him alone."

"He contravened an order and compromised our security."

"He stays right where he is."

Booker didn't push things any further at that point, and Wright, realizing his position, also let the issue drop. The fact that Booker had paid the fire bomber to change his aim that night never came up.

Later, as Wright considered how he was going to deal with a soldier who disobeyed orders without incurring the wrath of his second in command, he realized how tenuous his grip on PESQ was. In the military the superior has control over the life and death of a subordinate, and punishments are suffered without question. But PESQ members were volunteers in an underground group over whom Wright had no legal control. Push too hard and a disgruntled member might quit, taking his secrets with him. That would compromise security, and the house of cards would start to collapse.

Though usually dedicated to the details, Wright realized for the first time that he wasn't commanding a crack military unit, but rather a group of individuals, people with differing visions of how to get the job done. With that realization came the understanding that commanding this group of individuals had just gotten a lot more complicated. At a time when secrecy was more important than ever. Booker's insistence on not punishing the renegade worried him deeply.

Of course Booker would have no problem eliminating a renegade member to maintain order, Wright thought. He vowed to himself to not take that road, whatever happened.

***

As he ate his breakfast at John's Cantine Tuesday morning, Stubby could tell the Castonguay affair had stirred the pot the way he intended. The regulars couldn't get enough on the fire, and PESQ's existence had obviously been announced in a big way. After Rogers left Booker also contented himself with the thought that the bastard at the Granby Liar had finally served a useful purpose.

***

Faced with little new information, I decided to do a little calling around to see if anyone had ever heard of PESQ. Probably little more than a ragtag bunch of local rednecks, but I figured if PESQ was more than that maybe somebody in the English community would have heard something.

I started by calling area mayors with English names, then moved on to people like the local farmer's union representative, town clerks, and community organizations. People plugged into the community. I even called a few post offices, recognized in small towns as excellent sources of gossip.

In terms of actual facts about PESQ, I pumped hard and came up dry. I did get a few quotes that would serve as a piece on the English community's reaction to the fire. None of them openly advocated the approach taken by PESQ. However the mayor of East Farnham did go so far as to say that while he disagreed with the methods used, he understood the frustration that led to the existence of such a group.

"But we can't have people running around burning places down," he was quick to add. "We didn't like it when the FLQ did it and we don't like it now."

I finished off with a call to Hubert Perron, the local PQ organizer. He backed off a bit on the separatist rhetoric this time, but had little new to offer.

"Has anyone within the PQ ever heard of this terrorist group?" I asked, posing the question in a way that it would seem more sympathetic. Easier to attract flies with honey than with vinegar.

"No we have not," he replied.

"Do you have anyone investigating this on behalf of the party?"

"I have been in contact with the police several times," Perron replied in what I felt was a defensive tone. "But we are not detectives and we have no intention of becoming detectives."

"Doesn't this sound a bit like an English version of the FLQ?" I asked, more to set him up for a quote than to learn anything. The response was exactly what I expected.

"The Parti Québécois never supported the FLQ or any terrorist activity. We only advocate and work for the peaceful separation of Quebec from Canada."

I got the impression that even if this guy knew anything, he wasn't about to tell me, no matter how I asked the questions. I thanked him for his time and asked him to call me if he learned anything. He said he would, but I knew right away I'd never get a call from this man.

At a dead end, I did what every reporter does in this situation, I procrastinated. Steve Farnham was in early, so we visited about this and that. His main work in sports was usually over the weekend, so on a Tuesday he rarely appeared at the office. Sometimes he'd come in to straighten out some paperwork, if he had nothing better to do.

Just before noon I decided to let the story be for awhile and look at following up on the Tony Bakerstein murder. Of course any official police information for both the Bakerstein story and the Castonguay fire came from the same person: Fernand Dubois.

"I thought you were calling about the Castonguay fire," Dubois said in response to my first question. "That's what everybody else has been calling about. I must have taken 40 phone calls this morning."

"Don't worry, that comes next," I replied. "We'll do Bakerstein first."

"Just a second," Dubois said. I could hear him shuffling through some papers. Chances are the Bakerstein murder wasn't on the top of his pile of paperwork this morning.

"There's not much new that I can say right now," Dubois said after a few seconds. "Ballistics tests on the slugs taken out of the body have been completed, but we haven't yet connected them to a specific weapon. We have turned up a few leads, but the only other thing I can tell you is that the investigation is continuing."

Enough information for a short story, but nothing spectacular. The story of my day.

"Anything new about the Castonguay fire?"

"I'll tell you what I told the others: Not much new since yesterday. The investigation is continuing."

Damn. At least I still had two more days for something to break the logjam.

"I'll talk to you later," I said in a tone that showed my frustration.

"I'm sure you will," said Dubois in a tone that showed he enjoyed the influence he had over my work.

23

Wednesday and Thursday didn't come up much better than Tuesday had. I called a few prominent members of the French community, all of whom expressed varying degrees of fear, concern and anger at the prospect of English terrorists threatening the typically non-confrontational relations between the two language groups in the region.

With that and my earlier interviews I managed to cobble together a community reaction story for the Friday edition. It wasn't the story I wanted to write, but I had little else to go on. Friday's paper also contained my short follow-up on the Bakerstein murder, and a story on road accidents involving deer. Hunting season was on, and the deer were scrambling all over the place to get away from the hunters. The slightly bored sounding game warden I talked to said the sudden increase in deer-related accidents was an annual event.

It was about 3 p.m. Friday when I got the call. On the other end was a man with a voice full of gravel.

"I've got some information you might find interesting," the voice said. I could hear traffic in the background. Probably a pay phone.

"Okay, what have you got?" I replied.

"I know about a few things you've been digging into," the voice said. "Lots of things."

"Okay, what do you know?" I asked.

"I don't want to talk about this over the phone. If you want to talk we'll have to meet somewhere."

"I don't want to talk, I just want to listen," I said. "Are you sure we can't do this over the phone?"

"Not a good idea."

"Which thing is it that I've been looking into that you have information about?"

"For now let's just say it's important, and you'll kick your ass if you miss out on it," the man said.

"If you have all this information, why haven't you talked to the police?" I asked.

"I'm not out to get in any deeper. Do you want to know what the real story is or not?"

"Okay, where do you want to meet then?"

"Meet me in the parking lot of DuChene's bar in East Farnham at 7 o'clock tonight. Don't be late."

"How will we know each other?"

"Er, I'll recognize you."

Click. Dial tone.

I was left with a thrill of fear coursing through my chest and then grabbing my heart like a fist. I was going to meet my first secret informant. Not something I had expected to run into at a bush league paper like the Granby Liar.

The fist clutched onto my chest again that evening as I got ready for the meeting.

"Don't forget your cloak and dagger," joked Jen as I headed for the door.

"It's probably some crackpot who won't even show up," I replied. At that moment I found myself wishing my informant would be a no show, even though I really wanted the story.

The Falcon rumbled to life, its voice made a little deeper by an exhaust leak brought on by a particularly bad pothole earlier in the day. It looked like I was going to be back under the car Saturday, trying to do what I could to nurse a little more life out of the muffler.

The wind picked up as I pulled out of Brigham, headed for the parking lot of DuChene's, the bar where I'd pulled the stub of a cigar out of Fred Birches' throat after he and his drinking buddy scared the hell out of me in August. The fall leaves were mostly off of the trees now, and the wind whipped them around the car as I passed.

There were a surprising number of cars in the parking lot when I pulled in. Probably the after work crowd, I figured. Husbands who wanted a couple of beers to unwind before heading home to the wife and kids.

I parked next to a Vauxhall at the end of a row of cars, shutting off the engine and leaning back in my seat for a few seconds. From the bar I could hear a band setting up, a few guitar riffs here, some scattered drumming there, and the occasional "Check, one, two," over the PA. It

141

was promising to be a big night at the bar, and I even considered bringing Jen back after my meeting. We both loved live music, but hadn't been out for several weeks.

Two men came out of the side door of the bar, talking loudly. They looked my way, and then walked over.

"You got a light man?" the taller of the two men asked, a joint tucked behind his ear. His left hand leaned heavily on my rear view mirror.

"Sorry," I replied. "Lighter in the car doesn't work either."

"Time to sell your car," he replied. He and his friend moved on to the Vauxhall, got in and drove away.

I sat up in my seat as a signal flare orange GMC pulled into the yard. A large, heavyset man slowly climbed out. We made eye contact for a second before he turned his back and headed for the door.

I continued to wait for my informant.

***

Jen watched from the doorway as the Falcon pulled out of the driveway. She then went back inside, calling King in from the front yard. She didn't notice the blue Valiant parked facing the other way just past the post office.

About a minute later the Valiant came to life, rolling ahead slightly before pulling a U-turn. Behind the wheel was a large man with shaggy, curly hair. In the passenger seat was a thinner man with a hooked nose and US Marine-style brush cut. After checking to make sure they hadn't been seen already, both men pulled on ski masks, hiding the curly hair and the brush cut.

"Watch the dog, make sure he doesn't get out," the thin man said.

"You afraid of dogs or something?" the curly haired man said.

"Let's just keep it fast and simple."

The engine still running, the two men got out and casually walked to the door. Only one small frosted window. She'd have to open the door to see who it was. They knew this already. The thin man knocked.

"Mrs. Rogers?" he asked.

Jen only opened the door enough to see who it was, but it was still too much. The thin man stepped forward, pushing hard on the door with one hand, while reaching in and grabbing a handful of blonde hair with the other.

Jen screamed, but was unable to keep her balance. In one fluid motion she was pulled outside, hitting her cheek against the metal porch railing as she fell to the floor. The grip on her hair didn't let up as she heard the door slam shut behind her.

"You're gonna have to tell that man of yours to keep his nose outta things," the curly haired man whispered into her ear as the thin man pulled her up onto her knees. He was breathing hard and she could smell the cigarettes on his breath. "We're gonna make sure of that."

On the other side of the door King began barking frantically, knowing as dogs do when something is going terribly wrong. His claws dug at the door, tearing fine grooves into the hard wood.

"Please let me go," Jen pleaded.

"We're not done yet. We want to make sure you understand our message," said the thinner man, letting go of her hair and pushing her onto the floor of the porch.

Jen made a scramble for the door, but was kicked aside by the leather cowboy boots of the curly haired man. A second blow caught her in the ribs, while the third kick missed its mark as she stumbled to her feet, crouching. Unable to breathe properly and with the taste of blood in her mouth, she backed into the corner of the porch, her back against the railing.

"I understand your message, I really do," she said as the thinner man approached. He crouched down to look her in the eye, their faces only inches apart.

Jen could see veins in the whites of his eyes, a sharp contrast to the pale blue of the iris. The pupils were big, though one eyelid drooped a bit, a scar creasing it.

"I don't think you do understand. You're going to tell him that he'd be better off going back to the city where he belongs. You're going to tell him that bad things can happen to good people he cares about. And worse things will happen to the likes of him if he doesn't back off. So if he wants to save what's left of you after tonight, it's time to go."

Though trapped, Jen's adrenaline began to kick in, replacing the terror of the last few seconds with the instinct for survival. She knew she was trapped, that these men could do whatever they wanted. It made her mad. Behind the man she could hear King growling at the door, sniffing at the cracks as if it could bring him closer to those he needed to protect.

"You'd better remember everything I just said," he told her, reaching over and brushing some hair from her face. He noticed an instant too late that she wasn't shaking anymore.

In a swift motion Jen brought up her left hand, jamming her thumb into his right eye. She could feel the thumb as it pushed against the eyeball for an instant before it slid past it. Her right hand shoved him aside as he collapsed, howling in pain.

"You fucking bitch!" he screamed at her. "You're fucking dead now!"

Jen rushed for the door, but was hooked around the neck by the large arm of the curly haired man. His vice-like hold cut off her airflow, her arms and legs flailing about like a rag doll. With one arm clutching vainly at his muscular forearm Jen tried to poke at his eyes as well, but he calmly batted her free hand away. He then reached around and punched her in the lower back, making her scream in pain once again and slowing her efforts to get free.

Jen could feel the choke hold taking effect, gray spots appearing before her eyes. She kicked at the door, missing the mark. She kicked again, and missed.

"Please don't let that damn latch be caught," she thought to herself.

In a final, desperate act she pulled up her legs, putting all of her weight on his arm. The move pulled him forward and down slightly, as she put her feet down again and kicked for the door. The move gave her a few extra inches, and a bit of leverage as her bare foot planted itself solidly against the door. She pushed hard, hard enough to force her captor to step backwards.

But it also knocked the door open.

The next thing Jen saw was an extreme close-up of King's teeth as he sunk them into the arm that held her throat. The man staggered backwards, cursing in pain as the German Shepherd held on. With his free hand he punched vainly at the dog, whose teeth he could feel against the bones of his arm, severing flesh and muscle.

He kicked at the dog as he staggered backwards, catching it in the abdomen. The vice-like grip slackened for an instant, and he pulled his arm free. Jen fell to the floor, choking and gagging.

King lunged again, this time sinking his teeth into the closest available target, the large man's groin. The curly haired man squealed in pain, stumbling backwards and falling down the stairs of the porch. The big dog didn't let go, shaking his head and tearing at the denim and the flesh beneath.

"Sid, help me!" the large man called out, forgetting for that instant the need for secrecy.

Sid was still squirming on the porch floor, clutching his bleeding eye socket. He'd pulled off the ski mask and was using it to staunch the blood, which now covered the rest of his head in a macabre red mask of finger marks.

He stumbled to his feet, falling over the porch railing onto the lawn. Getting unsteadily to his feet he staggered drunkenly to the car. As he was doing so the larger man aimed another kick at the dog, with little effect. Then he reached down and grabbed the dog by the nose, prying the dog off of his groin.

As the teeth came off of his crotch they closed almost as quickly on the hand. The sharp pain reached a new level as he felt the last joint on his middle finger be forced out of place by the dog's molars.

"You fucker!" he groaned through clenched teeth. He didn't like being bested by a damn dog, but he knew it was time to get out. But he had to get it off of him first.

Suddenly, for an instant everything went black and it sounded like someone had fired a gun in his head. Jen had gotten to her feet and was now holding a long handled broom. Her first blow had caught him squarely in the side of the head. He could see her mouth moving, but couldn't make out the words.

As the second blow came around he put up his free arm, blocking the blow and clenching it under his arm. He yanked it free from Jen's grasp, and then turned it on the dog.

The first blow across King's head seemed to have little effect. The second caught him squarely in the ribs, knocking the wind out of him. He let go.

The man backed his way quickly to the car, using the broom to fend off the continued advances of the dog. He yanked open the driver's door, throwing the broom at the dog as he slammed it shut. King's claws raked down the side of the blue Valiant as it backed quickly out of the yard onto the street, smoking one tire as it took off up the street.

24

By 8 o'clock I figured my informant, whoever he was, had changed his mind about talking to me. To be sure I decided to give him another ten minutes before I headed for home.

During my hour-plus wait a few cars had left, and a few others had come in. Several people looked at me as they passed, probably more curious as to why some guy would be sitting in the parking lot by himself on a cool fall evening, rather than going in to listen to the music.

"Probably some guy waiting for a friend who's gone in to buy some dope." I imagined them thinking.

"So much for my secret informant," I said to myself as I fired up the Falcon. "I guess I was right when I told Jen it was some crackpot who probably wouldn't show."

I could see the police flashers as I crossed the train tracks coming into Brigham. But it took a few more seconds before I realized they were from two cruisers parked in front of my house.

"What's going on here," I called to one police officer as I ran across the lawn. "Where's my wife?"

"She's your wife?" the cop asked as he took a step to block my entry.

"Your damned right she is," I said, stepping around him while fighting back an urge to shove him aside. He didn't try to stop me.

"She's inside."

A second cop wearing gloves was examining the porch with a flashlight. I caught the sight of what looked like a blood smear. What in hell happened?

Inside Jen was sitting on the couch holding a damp rag to her cheek. On her left was a uniformed police officer, and on the right a plain clothes detective.

Jen sprung up from the couch when I came in, wrapping herself around me. Her face was hot and wet from crying, and the back of her dress was damp with perspiration despite the cool evening. She was shaking.

"What happened?" I asked.

Through the tears Jen told me the story of the attack. The knock at the door, the message for me, how she managed to get free before it got any worse. The police officers said nothing, examining their notes to see if this version had anything new to add to the story she'd already given them.

"Get someone to go look at the burn marks on the street from when the car left," the detective said to the uniformed officer afterwards.

When the Valiant left Jen called the dog in and locked the door. Unable to reach me, she called the police. They'd been at the house for about a half an hour before I got there.

"So who's after you?" asked the detective. "What have you been up to?"

"Just doing my job," I replied.

"And just what might that be?" he didn't know what I did.

"I'm a reporter for the Granby Leader-Mail," I told him.

"I've never seen your name there before," he said.

"You probably don't even read it," I replied, starting to feel like he thought I was some kind of outlaw.

"You're right there," he said, letting the matter drop.

The cops went back to asking Jen more questions for awhile before the detective was back to me. If I was a reporter, what had I been reporting on that would make somebody mad?

I listed off a few stories I'd been on lately, including the Bakerstein murder and the PESQ fire. Those last two were met by raised eyebrows and a flurry of note taking.

"Anything that stands out, any phone calls or messages before? Any warnings?" he asked.

"I had just gone to meet an informant, but he never showed up," I replied. "But I don't even know what he wanted to talk about."

It took me a few seconds before I remembered the "Rogers: Back Off" note given to Jen in early September and its twin a month later. He raised his eyebrows slightly.

"I never did figure out who they were from," I said after explaining the notes. "Sometimes we write things people don't like."

Forty minutes later the cops left, taking with them our statements, some blood samples from the porch, and a bloody thumb print from the railing.

"We'll have a car check on the house during the night," the detective said. It should have been comforting, but it wasn't.

"Dave, what in hell is going on here," Jen asked me after they left. "They nearly killed me."

I didn't want to think of that possibility, or the others that were flooding through my mind at that moment. The grisly images turned my stomach and made my face burn.

"They were just trying to scare us, that's all," it was a lie intended to calm her, and she picked up on that right away, pulling away from me.

"This is not how you scare people, this is how you hurt people," she said in a harsh tone, brushing her hair away from the cut on her cheek. Her eyes were red and glistening with water. She was right, and I knew it.

For the next two hours we talked, trying to figure out what to do next while dealing with the emotional aftermath of the night.

One thing was clear: Neither of us felt particularly safe sitting unarmed in our house. Sure, they weren't likely to come back tonight, but who knows? Maybe they'd want to get even for the gouged eye and the dog bites. It was Friday, so we decided to head back to the city for the weekend. We could surround ourselves with friends, hunker down and feel safe while we figured out what to do next.

Within minutes of that decision we had the car packed and King loaded into the back seat. He was limping a bit and one side seemed to be sore, but he was alert and apparently proud of his recent act of heroism. The tail wagged steadily and he couldn't bear to be away from us, not wanting to get separated again.

Fine by us. In my book, he'd just earned himself a lifetime supply of Dog Chow.

It was on the drive to the city that I really started to get mad. Once again they didn't have the balls to come after me, but opted to go after my wife instead. I was madder still that I didn't even know who it was that was pissed and why.

Then my thoughts went to Rachel and the others at the office telling me how no one ever went after the reporters, no matter how mad they were. Great advice that was.

I tried to hide my rage in the car, which made me silent. Jen hated seeing me mad, even when I had good reason to be. She picked up on the silence.

"I'm mad too, you know," she said.

"I just wish I knew who to be mad at," I said. "I don't even know who to go after."

"You're not 'going after' anyone," Jen said.

"What am I supposed to do, quit my job? What paper would hire a guy who ran away from some threats he got at his last job?"

"You're not a cop, and you're not some cowboy, so just drop it," Jen said.

I decided it was time to drop it, knowing full well my questions still needed to be answered. If I at least knew who attacked Jen and why, maybe I'd be able to figure out what to do. I'd get the last word. I always get the last word.

We spoke little for the rest of the hour-long trip. Traffic was light, the only thing slowing us down were the stops at the toll booths, as we fished around for quarters.

Just before 1 a.m. Saturday morning we pulled in to the alley next to Jen's mother's place in the Notre Dame de Grace neighborhood of Montreal. Her large apartment was typical of the neighborhood, in a row of three-floor blocks separated by narrow driveways. My mother in law lived on the top floor.

We had already decided not to tell her about what happened, at least not yet. Best to say we decided to come in at the last minute. We were tired and not ready to have her panicking in the middle of the night. But she spotted the cut on Jen's cheek.

"What happened to you?"

"I fell and whacked my face on the porch railing," Jen replied, a partial truth. Her mother glanced at me and I winced at the thought that she might think I had something to do with it. Though she was always nice to me and Jen said otherwise, I always suspected she thought of me as an intruder. The one who was sleeping with her daughter.

"That was one hell of a fall," she said. "Let me get a look at that," she said, grabbing her by the chin and turning the bruise towards the light.

"It's fine mother. I've looked at it already," Jen replied, pulling away. She was looking to change the subject. "Where's daddy?"

"He's at a sales conference in Ottawa. He'll be back Sunday," she replied. She got the hint about changing the subject, but continued to eye both of us suspiciously. We decided to let her stew until the morning.

My sleep that night was filled with violent dreams where I was helpless to react. A world filled with violence which, despite my best efforts, I could do nothing about. Feelings I hadn't been able to deal with when I was awake came to the fore. I could see my father in the mix of faces, but he was neither aggressor nor victim. Just watching.

And each time I woke up I felt worse than the time before.

Three hours after we went to bed I was laying there, watching Jen in the pale light of the early morning. The area around the cut had taken on a purplish hue, and stood out from her cheek.

The more I thought the more the rage built in me. I woke up feeling like a victim, but this was being replaced by a slow, cold rage that welled up from the pit in my stomach and pushed the fear out of my heart.

The problem was I had no idea who to vent my rage against. Hard to carry out a vendetta when you have no idea who should be on the receiving end. You can't kill shadows, and the night's disturbing dreams clouded things even further. A bit like a punch drunk boxer who's still standing, still swinging, but can't see his opponent.

I was going to find my opponent, and I was going to get even.

The floor was cold when my feet hit it. The landlord controlled the hot water heating, and in October he only fired up the boiler during the day. Not many people were up at 6 a.m. on a Saturday morning. The hardwood floors creaked as I made my way from what had once been Jen's room, down the narrow hallway to the kitchen. If possible, the linoleum in the tiny kitchen felt even colder.

Jen came from a family of coffee drinkers, so I put on the first pot of the day. Mother in law would be up soon. That woman never seemed to sleep.

I grabbed an old wool blanket that was hanging over the back of a chrome kitchen chair to throw over my shoulders against the morning chill. A glance out the window revealed the beginnings of a grey, overcast day, the sky seeming to blend in to the city. The St. Lawrence River couldn't be seen from here, but I knew it would be covered in a thick layer of fog.

Faced with an unplanned trip to the city, I decided to visit my mom. She lived alone in an apartment on Côte-des-Neiges, where she'd lived ever since I struck out on my own a few years ago. Born and raised in the country, she had developed a network of friends and activities over the years, and seemed to be constantly busy.

I left Jen with her mother at about 10 o'clock, taking more time to fume over yesterday's events. Jen was quiet, subdued. I knew there was going to be some serious discussion between us about what was going to happen next. She hadn't said anything yet, but I knew that at this moment she didn't like the idea of ever being alone in our house. Hell, I didn't like the idea very much myself.

The thought of getting a gun crossed my mind. But hell, neither of us had ever used one, so who was I kidding? One of us would probably end up shooting the Avon Lady or something.

I walked down to the Vendôme metro station, and caught the orange line up to Snowdon. After last night's events in the country, the fluorescent lights and stale air of the metro felt strangely reassuring. From Snowdon it was a short walk to Côte-des-Neiges and over to the red brick triplex overlooking Kent Park.

I've always had a good relationship with my mother. Partly because we had to rely on each other after my dad died. Though we both stayed off the thornier issues like sex or drinking, we regularly turned to each other for advice. Still, part of me was hesitant to tell her what had happened to Jen. When I'd gotten the job at the Granby Liar she'd seemed less enthusiastic than I'd expected. Now add the prospect of danger to myself and Jen (that's the order she would have put things in), and I knew it wasn't going to be an easy conversation.

She was surprised to see me at the door, and I didn't let on right away why I was in the city unexpectedly. We started by talking about the things she'd been up to, the trials and tribulations of friends of the family. I'd been in the country for much of the last five months, with only the occasional weekend visit to the world I'd called my own for most of my life. But the subject came up.

"When you called the other night I thought you said you weren't coming in this weekend," she said. A tone in her voice showed she thought something was up.

I decided to bite the bullet, giving her an abridged version of what happened. I skipped the worst parts, though it was hard to avoid the fact that Jen and I had been on the receiving end of some very serious threats. No mother likes to hear that.

"I never liked you going back there," she muttered, almost under her breath. She got up and walked into the kitchen, obviously deep in thought.

"This could have happened anywhere," I replied. "Worse things happen in here every day."

From the kitchen she said something I couldn't hear.

"What?"

"Not to you."

I decided to take the bull by the horns.

"Ma, it's pretty obvious that you didn't like the idea of me working out there. You never encouraged it, but you got all excited the time I had a shot at that Montreal Star job. What's so bad about the country?"

Despite the events of the last 24 hours, I'd started to get attached to the area. I knew I wasn't staying at the Granby Liar forever, but this was the area where my ancestors had lived, and the people had, with a few exceptions, been welcoming.

She walked back into the living room, her face tense, pensive. Then the expression changed. A decision had been made.

"I love the country. I miss it every day. It's that Stubby Booker."

25

Those four words hung in the air for a few seconds, like beads of water on a tightly woven carpet, reluctant to sink in. They confirmed what until this moment I had only thought of as a wild speculation. Paranoia.

"What do you mean?" I asked.

"There's a history there," she said. It was obvious that her chest was tight, like that feeling shy people get when addressing a group. The words had to be forced out.

"I think it's time for a history lesson," I said. "I'm listening."

As I said before, she had always refused to discuss why we came to the city in the first place. Now she had opened the door, and I was determined to stick my foot in there.

"Your father wasn't exactly an angel when he was younger," she said. A pause as she searched for the words.

"I'd heard that," I said.

"You knew about the moonshine business your grandfather was into. Your dad was into it too, and when those days came to an end, he missed the excitement of running some kind of scam or other. Nothing serious. He was a good man, he just liked the thrill of it all, I guess."

"Stubby Booker was a friend of his. They met as kids when your grandfather was running his still. As you know the farm was only a few miles from the border, and Stubby used to stay there when he was running booze across the line. They were just boys, and like I said your father liked the thrill of it all."

"By the time your father and I met, Stubby had moved on to bigger and better things, and your grandfather had passed away. The moonshining days were over, and your dad was settling down. He liked the thrill of the border runs, but he was no criminal. He stayed out of the illegal stuff, but he was still friends with Stubby."

She got up and walked into the kitchen, putting the kettle on the stove for another coffee. Her steps were slow, labored. Carrying the weight of difficult memories.

"One day your father came home, and it was obvious something was wrong. He would pace around the house, then get up and leave. A few

154

minutes later he'd be back, then he'd be gone again, wandering around the barnyard."

"I must have asked him what was wrong a dozen times that day, but he wouldn't say anything."

"About a week later he comes to me with this wild idea. We would move to Montreal and he'd get a job there. Maybe he could get a construction job, make some real money. Get away from the drudgery of the farm."

"I knew something was wrong. The farm may not have been the most exciting life we could have chosen, but I knew your father loved it. We had a good life there, and while your father may have liked a little excitement now and then, that farm was his sanctuary. Still, he refused to say what was wrong."

"Personally I didn't care where we were. I had you and I had him, and that's all I needed. I decided to avoid the immediate conflict and let it drop," she said. "But we always talked about things, and I knew it had to come out eventually."

"About a week later your father was getting ready to go to Farnham and catch the train to the city, to find an apartment and maybe even a job. He never did like driving in traffic. I decided that before he committed to anything, I had to know what was wrong."

"We don't keep secrets, you know that," I said. "You're not going anywhere until we talk."

"The train leaves in an hour, and it's a half-hour to Farnham," he replied.

"Plenty of time to tell me what's going on. Otherwise, you're not going anywhere," I said.

"He tried to fight it. He even got mad, but your father never would have threatened me for anything. Then he unloaded the burden that had been on his mind, that had robbed him of his sleep. He gave me only the barest of details, enough to convince me to let him go that day. By the time we'd moved to the city, I'd gotten most of it, but I never did get it all. It's a burden that I've carried ever since, and that has shaped all our lives."

"Your father had been in Roxton Pond, visiting Stubby. As I said Stubby was into bigger and better things, while your father had left the moonshine business behind. But they were still close friends, and kept their history between them. Apparently your father showed up at the wrong time."

"I swore to myself you'd never know."

She paused, staring at the wall. She may have been searching for the right words, but from where I was sitting she was just drawing things out. This had been kept from me all my life, and now she seemed to be stalling. Though I wanted to shake it out of her, I kept my cool.

"That day your father dropped by Stubby's for a visit. No one was in the house, so he began checking around the outbuildings. That's when he heard the shot."

"He found Stubby standing over a body. Turns out it was a police officer," she said. "Your father was in the worst place at the worst possible time."

"Stubby got your father to help him bury the body out in the woods. Your father objected, but Stubby started by reminding him of their long friendship. He refused, and then Stubby started making threats. Dave was dealing with an armed man who had just killed a cop, so he knew he didn't have much choice in the matter."

"By the time we were ready to move to the city, we'd worked out a plan. Everybody was talking about the missing police officer, and nobody suspected Stubby. We managed to quietly move to Montreal without too many questions. Probably because we only took what we could fit on the pickup truck. We didn't give out our new address to anyone, save your grandmother."

"As soon as we were set up here, your father went back to the police with a lawyer. At first they wanted to arrest him as an accessory to the murder, but his lawyer managed to work out a deal. He would testify against Stubby, and they would drop the charges against him."

"When they arrested Stubby they went to the spot your father told them about, but there was no body. It was obvious a hole had been filled in, but when they dug it out there was nothing there. Stubby had moved the body."

"At first they tried to get it out of your father, figuring he was up to something. Then they tried to get it out of Stubby, and of course that didn't work. The police knew he'd done it, but with no body, they couldn't do a thing."

"In the end Stubby was convicted of obstruction of justice, and sentenced to ten years in prison. We were told he'd be out on parole in four. Our plan was for your father to work in the high steel for most of that time so we could save our money. Just before his release we were going to pack up and move again, this time far away. Saskatchewan was the plan, but your father died before we got there."

There was a silence in the apartment. This was a lot of information to take in all at once, and now, with it out in the open, neither of us knew what to say. Questions I'd had for years had finally been answered, but I didn't like the answers I'd been given.

For the first time Stubby Booker ceased to be an academic curiosity. He was no longer just the small town crimes boss, the guarantee of a good story to write the next time he had a run in with police. He was the man responsible for my family's exile. My parents had lived in a world of stress caused by this vile man while I, as a young boy, went through life oblivious to it all.

Confusion would best describe my state of mind for the next few minutes. Everything had changed and nothing had changed, and I couldn't grasp what it all meant. Long standing questions had finally been answered, but only spawned more questions. I had always suspected something unpleasant, but nothing like this. Too much information.

"So dad was an outlaw," I said, more to myself than to my mother.

"He was a good man," she said. "He liked excitement when he was younger. Your father never hurt anyone. Not like that bastard Stubby."

Her use of the word "bastard" shocked me, because foul language wasn't a normal part of her vocabulary. I could feel her deep-seated hatred of Stubby Booker. In the mind of a woman who became a widow too soon, he was the man responsible for forcing them out of their home, responsible for her husband taking a job in high steel in the city. A job that had killed him. Responsible for the path her life had taken for the last quarter century.

"How come you never moved back?" I asked.

"It was too difficult. I'd settled here by then, made new friends. And after your father testified and his name was in the papers he'd been pretty much branded as one of Stubby's fellow outlaws. I didn't want you to grow up with that around your neck. Besides, I didn't want to live in the same area as that awful man. I thought I saw him on the street once, and it filled me with such sheer terror I came home and cried."

We sat in silence for a few minutes. A silence between a mother and a son who had been through a lot together, supporting each other along the way with little more than their existence. At that moment nothing needed to be said, even though there was still a lot to think about.

The silence was shattered by the sound of the phone. It was one of those wall mounted rotary models, like you often saw in a workshop or a garage.

"Hello," my mother said. "Yes he is. Just a moment please."

She handed me the receiver with a shrug, showing she had no idea who it was.

"Dave, I've been searching all over hell for you. You've got a problem." It was Harry Bankroft.

"Someone burned your house down last night."

26

Already pushed to my limits by my mother's revelations, I had a hard time taking in what Bankroft said. Kind of like when you're being told something important when you're drunk. The words are there and you understand them, but they still don't sink in, don't have an immediate effect. Fail to generate any kind of emotional response.

"What?" I said, unable to muster up anything better.

"Our freelancer, what's his name. Aww shit, can't remember his name again. Anyways he was listening to his scanner again last night when the call came in. He called me when he got there and realized whose house it was. At first we thought you must have been inside. Once we figured out you were gone we told the cops and started calling around. I didn't have any of your numbers in the city."

"How bad?" the only words I could force out of my dry mouth.

"Bad enough. They did manage to save some of it, but you won't be living there anytime soon, if ever. I'm afraid you've lost most of your stuff."

There was a silence on the line, neither of us sure what to say next. Bankroft made the next move.

"You'd better get out here," he said.

"Yeah," I said. I felt dizzy.

I told my mother quickly and her face blanched. First the attack on Jen, then a few hours later, this.

"Thank God you weren't there," she said.

"I've got to go," I said. "I don't want to tell Jen on the phone."

The trip back to the mother-in-law's, while barely more than fifteen minutes, was surreal. I was still trying to grasp the situation, asking myself if I hadn't in some way misunderstood Bankroft. Maybe it was all some sort of hallucination, or a dream. It didn't seem real. I found myself wishing it was a delusion, that it would be better that I was crazy for thinking my house had been burned down. Then I could just give my head a shake and get on with life. But as the trip progressed and my mother-in-law's front door got closer the reality set in.

159

Like most of the important things in my life, it became real when I told Jen.

"Why would anyone do this?" she said, pleading for an answer, her eyes moistening. "Dave, what in Hell is going on?"

I gave her a quick rundown of my family history, and the blocks began to fall into place. Of course we couldn't prove that Stubby Booker was out to get me, but the circumstantial evidence was pretty convincing. None of it pointed anywhere else.

We left King in the city. He was stiff from the aftermath of the previous evening, but otherwise none the worse for wear. He seemed to walk with a little more dignity, perhaps pride in knowing he'd protected Jen when she needed it most. He whined at the door when we left, unwilling to give up his guard duties just yet.

The drive back to Brigham was fraught with tension, each of us wanting to see the damage, to see what we could save. We had just begun thinking of Brigham as home, and now we didn't have a place to live there. Homeless in our new home.

I pushed the Falcon up to around 75, the best I felt I could do without killing it. This wasn't the time for a breakdown. I thought of that night in the summer when I had been chased by the drunks on the way home from the bar. A hint of doubt about Booker, about the reality of the whole situation returned. In the back of my mind I knew I was going to need two things: Proof against Booker and a plan.

Right now I had neither. But I was going to have to deal with more immediate concerns. By the time we crossed the tracks in Brigham I could smell the smoke. The fire was out, but the stench of burnt building still hung in the village, held there by heavy air on a still morning.

The house was mostly still there, blocked off with yellow police barricade tape. The outer structure was three-quarters intact. From the look of things someone had smashed in the living room window and set the place on fire. I hadn't covered that many fires, but it was obviously deliberate.

The police had gone, at least for the time being, and there were only two firefighters on the scene. They sat on the scorched front porch, chatting and smoking cigarettes, just like they owned the place. The familiarity of these strangers with my home was disturbing.

After we identified ourselves they let us inside. The living room was destroyed, and they warned us out of the room. The blaze had weakened the floor, and it wasn't safe. The kitchen was heavily water damaged, and looked as if it had been attacked by vandals. High pressure hoses can wreak havoc on a tidy room.

We said nothing to each other, rummaging around in silence. Occasionally one of us would pick up something, an artifact of our life at this house, only to put it back down. The thought of having to sift through everything that had made up our life was overwhelming. Too much had happened in the last 24 hours, and we were both numb.

The heavy stench of house smoke was everywhere, a sharp, tangy smell that is different from a regular wood fire. Within a few minutes we smelled almost as bad as the house. I remembered the look on Raoul Castonguay's face the night his home burned, and figured we must look the same right now.

For the most part the bedroom wasn't too badly wrecked. The walls had black streaks and our clothes would all have to be washed. Luckily our most precious keepsakes, like the Rogers family Bibles, had been kept in a closet there. Booker hadn't managed to take everything away from us.

And he wasn't going to take away anything more, I swore to myself. Even though at that moment I felt powerless, clueless, and at the mercy of forces beyond my control.

We were sitting on the hood of the Falcon staring blankly at the house when the cops showed up again. The sun was shining, but a cold wind reminded us that winter wasn't far off. A detective in a trench coat, the same one I'd first met the night before when I got set up with my secret meeting, walked calmly towards us. The second police officer was Fernand Dubois, dressed in jeans and a leather jacket. It was the first time I'd seen him out of uniform, and it looked odd. Kind of like when you see a politician on a construction site wearing a hard hat, or in a cheese factory wearing a hair net.

"What brings you out here?" I asked Dubois after the niceties were out of the way.

"You're one of my best customers," the provincial police flak replied. "I wanted to know if it has any connection to anything we've talked about."

In the back of my head I knew he was there more out of personal curiosity than anything. But I was beyond caring. Let him look.

The detective cut to the point. Where were we after the attack? Why did we leave? Did we see anything before we left that seemed suspicious? Montreal. Didn't feel safe here. No.

I decided to give him the quick rundown on the Stubby Booker connection. His eyebrows raised a few times, but I got little other reaction. He was quick with a response after I finished.

"Not much for proof there," he said. "We will keep it in mind though as the investigation continues. Right now we're looking more at getting the two guys who were here last night."

Though I was already pretty sure, I decided to ask the detective how the fire was set. My initial analysis proved to be correct.

"Whoever did this didn't waste any time," he said. "They just walked up and threw a fire bomb through the living room window. We do have a witness saying they saw a car drive away, but it was dark and they couldn't see what kind or what colour. Basically all we know is the approximate time. About midnight."

It turns out the neighbor who saw the car also spotted the fire and called for help. That's why they managed to save as much of the house as they did. Thank God for good neighbors. Though I never did find out which neighbor it was, or how they happened to be watching outside at that hour. Every small town has someone like that, awake at all hours, watching, always watching.

That was pretty much it for the cops. We now had to figure out a number of things: Where do we live now? How do we replace the things we lost? How do we clean up the things we could save? What do we do in the meantime?

Added to the pain in the ass side of things was the fact we had no insurance. What was lost was lost, and with our already tight budget, we wouldn't be replacing it anytime soon. No TV, no living room furniture, and good luck washing the smell of smoke out of whatever else we could salvage.

On top of that neither of us felt particularly safe. Sure, we could find a new place, and then Booker's thugs would find us there and do God knows what. Jen's first reaction was that we should just pack up what we

162

had left and go back to the city. My journalistic career would have to be put on hold for awhile until I could scratch up something better.

I wished the whole situation would just go away.

But it wouldn't just go away. In the back of my head I knew that even if I tucked my tail between my legs and went back to Montreal, it would never really go away.

27

Jen and I sat there on the hood, discussing what to do until the sun began to make its way into the trees in the west. It was chilly, but it was only when the light began to fade that we noticed.

Several times cars passed, slowing down to see the remains of our house. We stared, sure it was our arsonists, but as far as we could tell they were only curious neighbors. Then a small brown Austin Mini pulled up. It was Harry Bankroft.

"Let's get out of this town and get some coffee," he said. "Not much point sitting here."

We loaded into his tiny car, me in the front and Jen in the back. She sat crossways, making the most of the space available. Bankroft pushed the Mini up to around 60 as we headed up des Érables, and before long both of us were looking for someplace to hold on. Jen and I remained silent, fixated on the road, while Bankroft kept up a steady stream of dialogue on anything that seemed to come to his overactive mind.

Ten minutes later we were at the Roma Pizzeria in Cowansville. I caught myself scanning the room as we walked in, evaluating the faces. We ordered coffee, and since we were there, pizza.

"So what have you done to deserve this?" he asked, apparently an attempt to lighten the situation.

"I'm not really sure," I said. "Though there is a possibility that it has something to do with Stubby Booker."

I felt silly mentioning it. Like I was just being paranoid. After all, I had no real proof, just some interesting family history to retell. I gave Bankroft the short version.

He was silent for a moment, staring at me.

"So you're saying that your dad squealed on the local crime boss, and now, twenty-whatever years later he has it in for you? How interesting."

I felt sillier than ever.

"I just found this out," I said. "It seems to be the only thing that makes sense. The others write about Booker and nothing happens. I write about him and my wife gets beat up and my house gets burned down."

"And you couldn't have pissed off anyone else?" a logical question from Harry.

164

"Not this seriously, I don't think."

"These are serious people," Jen said.

"I know," Bankroft said, surveying the cut on her cheek, which, despite a bit of makeup was now surrounded by a purple tinge. "I'm just skeptical by nature."

"What about PESQ?" he asked.

"I thought of that, but burning out an English guy doesn't seem to be their way of doing things."

"You'd think so," he replied. "Then again, maybe it wasn't the flavour they'd hoped for."

Our pizza arrived, and for a few minutes we concentrated on eating. We hadn't had time for lunch, and breakfast didn't amount to much for either of us.

"You'd better take a few days off and get yourselves organized," Bankroft said a few minutes later. "Salvage your stuff and find a new place to live."

"We don't really have the cash for me to be taking time off," I replied.

"That's not a problem. Take the time you need."

Harry was right. We were essentially homeless, with little money and no clue of where we were going to live, or how we were going to replace what we lost in the fire. On top of that October was almost over. Though we probably had another month before winter set in, frost had already cloaked the fields.

On top of that was the safety issue. I knew I wasn't going to feel comfortable letting Jen out of my sight. She'd been attacked, and I hadn't been there to defend her. Part of me felt like a failure, unable to protect my family when I was supposed to. It helped to fuel my growing anger against Booker.

"Check in now and then so we know what's going on." Bankroft said when he dropped us off in Brigham. He backed the little Austin Mini into the street and drove off, leaving a little puff of blue smoke when he changed gears.

We had already decided that we were going to spend the night at Jen's mother's place. After all, we had nothing out here, and right now it just didn't feel safe. Now that I had been given some time off, we'd probably spend a couple of days regrouping, figuring out what to do next.

The immediate problem would be explaining this to Jen's mother. I always felt she thought I was just some hoodlum and that her daughter would get hurt being married to me. The fact that my late father had been best friends with the local crime boss wouldn't help things.

Our discussions continued on the trip back in. Jen was pretty set on having me turn tail and run. I was pretty set on getting even, though I had no idea how. Squaring off against an armed criminal wasn't very appealing. It didn't make much sense no matter how you looked at it.

Boiled down, the conversation went something like this:

Jen: "We can't go back there. You're definitely not going back there."

Me: "You can't go back there. I have to."

My mother-in-law was given the full story when we got back that night. We let it all hang out, the beating, the fire, the apparent reasons for it all. It pretty much cemented her already well set opinion of me. She didn't say it outright, but there were a few glances that let me know she wouldn't object if I walked out of her daughter's life forever. She didn't object nearly as strongly as Jen when I mentioned going back – alone.

28

Getting Jen to accept my going back to work, and the Townships, was no easy task. In fact she never really accepted it. Every relationship develops its sore spots over the years, and for us this is one of those sore spots that never entirely went away. Just when you think it's gone it creeps back, like the bad smell of a sideways glance, a carefully placed, or misplaced word that reminds you it hasn't gone anywhere, and never will.

Monday morning I drove to work from Montreal, and was at my desk by 10 a.m. I tried to make it seem like a typical workday, but inside I was paralyzed with fear. What in hell was I doing? Run away you idiot. I stared at the newspapers, trying to keep it all together.

I had little trouble getting Bankroft to OK my sleeping on the couch in the newsroom. It had been done before by homeless reporters. I promised I'd get a place to stay as soon as I could.

But I was a pack of nerves. In an office where the phones never stopped, my heart jumped every time one rang. When the main door slammed I had to look around to see who it was. My mouth was dry all day. My appetite was gone. I dreaded the coming of the night.

"Isn't vagrancy against the law?" Steve Farnham making a joke. It fell flat. A couple of others tried to joke about it. Almost everyone stopped by my desk to say how bad they felt about the attack, and the house, and Jen. I squirmed uncomfortably in my chair. I felt like a criminal awaiting trial; bound to a process that could only have one possible, unfortunate end. There was little in the way of light at the end of this tunnel.

The night was just what I expected it would be: Cold, dark, spooky. The factory was silent except for the occasional creaks and groans of an old building that had seen better days. The furnace had been fired up for the first time to push out the fall chill, and the place smelled of the sharp, chemical tang of fuel oil. The ducts echoed the complaints of the furnace fan, with its slipping belt emitting the occasional sharp squeal into the darkness.

I got up a few times to make the rounds, armed with a baseball bat and flashlight. I wasn't sleeping anyway, and it helped pass the time. By 4 a.m. I fell into a fitful slumber, only to be awakened two hours later by the janitor. He seemed almost as scared as I did. Of course he was looking at a half-awake homeless man with a flashlight and a bat, hair on end and eyes wide with fear. After a brief greeting and an explanation of why I was there he went about his work. That was pretty much it for my night's sleep.

For the next couple of days I did my best to pretend it had all been a bad dream. Business as usual. I even did a story about a haunted house near Brigham as a teaser for Halloween. Seems every time a train passed by a light could be seen in the barn, coming outside and entering the house. As the train rolled through the front yard people on the road could see the light go from the kitchen upstairs and then go out. The mystery had endured for a half century, and some skeptical scholar from McGill was out trying to figure it out.

After the first couple of days I became pretty good at pushing Stubby Booker out of my mind, at least for short periods. I even managed to eat a little. But sleep was still lacking. So was a plan. Jen checked in every day, saying little, I could tell, of how she was really feeling. Every call ended with a plea for me to come back home. On the Wednesday night I did, grabbing some quarters off Rachel's desk for the tollbooths. I needed a break, a shower and a decent night's sleep.

No such luck. The dreams came back. This time my father was frantically digging a hole. Sweat poured off his face, forcing him to stop occasionally to wipe it from his eyes.

"It's got to be here!"

"It's too late dad," my voice is soft, calm. A polar opposite to his frantic words.

"No it's not!"

"It's been dug up already."

"No it hasn't! I saw him bury it here!"

"It's not there dad. No one knows where it is."

"HE knows where it is!"

"Yes dad. But we don't."

"Where in Hell is it?"

"You lost it."

***

Thursday morning I was back in the office. It was Halloween.

Rachel and Harry stayed late that evening, ready to cover any Halloween-related problems. Mat night had gone off without a hitch, but something, a fire, some vandalism, always happened on Halloween. A few kids came by the office for candy. By 10 o'clock the press run was done, the papers ready for the trucks. The police scanner was silent. Rachel and Harry went home, and I locked the door behind them.

Like any grown adult who's been traumatized, I left the light on my desk switched on. It did nothing to increase my safety, but it felt reassuring. I dozed off at midnight. Not long after I awoke to see a gorilla standing next to my desk. He was staring at me. Then a large hand went over my face.

Thrashing out with arms and legs I think I did manage to get a shot at someone. I tried to suck breath through the clenched fingers, and the sweet, biting chemical smell of ether entered my lungs. Fear bit through the haze as I thrashed again, but only for a few seconds. Then darkness closed in around me, smothering me like a blanket.

The cold, corrugated steel of the van floor cut through the haze. The smell of ether filled my nostrils and bile coated my tongue. I kicked out, thrashing around in the empty compartment. My hands were tied.

"Just relax," grumbled a calm, steady voice. The haze lifted a little further. A work boot was next to my face. We hit a bump, train tracks I think. My head bounced off the floor, scattering what was left of the haze. I brought my legs around and sat up. The bile taste in my mouth was replaced by the coppery taste of blood.

The body connected to the work boot snapped on a long handled flashlight, right in my face. Nothing but glare from where I sat.

"Must've bit your lip," the voice said. The rag, still smelling of ether, was wiped across my face, stinging as it passed.

I said nothing. In my head I was asking God to let me see my wife again. Anything for that. That's all that mattered. Fear pushed out all other sensations, pounding the blood through my ears. The sweat trickling down my back a sharp contrast to the cool air of late fall.

"Don't worry, we're not about to kill you or anything," the voice again. I'd heard that voice before, but I couldn't quite place it.

"What in hell is going on here?" I said. I tried to sound enraged, but my voice wavered at the end, sounding more scared than sure. Not yet ready to trust the words of the man who had just abducted me.

We passed under a streetlight, which cast a faint glow through the rear windows, the only ones in the van. My abductor was wearing a sheet over his head, like a ghost, or a member of the Ku Klux Klan. Looking forwards I could see the gorilla was driving.

The gorilla hit the brakes and veered left, sending me sliding across the floor. The hood with the familiar voice balanced himself with a leg. He was sitting on the wheel well, and seemed to be looking at the wall of the van, lost in thought. A right, and then another left. I tried to figure out from the turns and stops where we were, but quickly realized it was pointless. The van stopped. The one with the hood opened the back doors and stepped out, turning to beckon me outside. Through my own pounding heart I could hear the sound of a rushing stream.

The moon was out, casting a pale light. Shit, I'm on Miltimore Road. This is where they found Tony Bakerstein. Please let me see my wife again. Please, shit, please, fuck, fuck, fuck.

"I think you've been here before," said the Ghost. "At least you've written about it. Tony Bakerstein came here once. Makes you wonder about spirits, this time of year and all. I wonder if he's still here."

For the first time I noticed the cold, and the fact I was in a T-shirt. Frost coated the guardrails and glistened off the gravel in the moonlight. Ghost untied my hands and threw me my sneakers.

"I just do the stories, that's my job," I said, fumbling with the laces and feeling how the frost had stiffened the ground with my bare foot. I'd managed to regain my composure, keep my voice steady. Act like I wasn't about to break down and beg for mercy. But the "It's just my job" line felt pretty weak.

"That's what we're counting on," said Gorilla, his first words. "Do your job. With a little help."

"What kind of help?"

"We're going to give you a little scoop. A month ago Tony was brought here, much like you were. The difference is he was shot several times with a long-barreled .38. That .38 was seized in a police raid at Stubby Booker's place a few days later. Pretty soon the police are going to make the connection and Booker's going to be arrested for murder."

"And then you want me to write the story."

"No, here's the special part. We want you to finish the story now, before he gets arrested. Make your own ending."

"I can't do that," I said. "I can't write about things that haven't happened yet. Besides, wouldn't that piss off a lot of people, including the police and the guy who wants to ruin my life?"

"This guy is out to get you. Don't you want to get even?" Gorilla asked.

"I want to get even, but pissing him off even more isn't going to settle the score. There has to be more. Why don't I just wait for the arrest?"

"Simple enough. He wants you dead. We want him dead. As long as he's alive he's a threat. Remember that Simson kid? He said Booker's name in court once and he wound up dead. How do you think that happened?"

My mouth went dry. My shirt was sticking to my body in spite of the cold. What in hell had I gotten myself into? I looked around, seeing little in the way of a useful escape route or weapon. It was obvious I wasn't going anywhere unless these guys gave me the green light. That wasn't going to happen unless they got what they came for. My best shot at staying alive was to play along.

"So what's the point of writing ahead of time that Stubby Booker has been arrested for murder?" I asked.

Gorilla answered from somewhere in the darkness: "We didn't say write a story, we said finish a story."

There was a pause as gorilla struggled with his mask to light a cigarette. Yes, here I was in the middle of nowhere with a smoking primate, and yet the situation wasn't the least bit amusing.

"We know about your father and Stubby," Gorilla said. "We know they were friends, and that your father saw something he shouldn't. We're guessing that you've figured that part out."

"Yeah, so?"

"But your father left, went to work in high steel with the plan of getting his family out of harm's way. Then he fell."

I said nothing. Gorilla took a drag off the cigarette.

"Actually he didn't fall. He was pushed. Under orders from Stubby Booker."

My ears rang. My chest tightened. I stumbled slightly as I walked to the guardrail, a new layer of sweat coming out on my forehead. That sensation of hearing something but not being able to fully grasp its meaning returned. Gorilla handed me his cigarette. Without thinking, I, the non-smoker, took it. The world began to spin and next thing I knew, I was laying on the ground, the surface layer of gravel sticking to my face as I struggled to get up. Neither of them tried to help me.

"The way we see it, he wants you dead, and he'll do that sooner or later. It won't matter if he's in jail or not. You've seen that. You have to get rid of him."

"You want me to kill him?" I said, feeling a bit like I was watching a movie.

"It's up to you," piped in Ghost, speaking for the first time. A tone in his voice also sounded familiar, but I couldn't place it. "This man killed your father, and he wants to kill you. Maybe even people close to you. Do you have a choice?"

At that moment it didn't seem like it.

"You can't expect me to just go and kill someone," I said in a tone that betrayed how bewildered I was. "I mean, uh, people don't just do stuff like that."

"Who in hell are you guys anyway? Why should I believe you any more than I'd believe Booker?"

"Because you know it's true," Ghost said.

"We're done talking," Gorilla said, walking to the van with a slight limp. "Let's go."

Neither of them spoke on the return trip to Granby. I asked questions but got no answers. Just silence as their words seeped into my consciousness. The reality that I was trapped into a game that I never created, that I never wanted, that I couldn't even fully understand. Facing the prospect of going after a man who had taken my father from me, my home from me, and apparently was out to take away everything I had or was ever going to have. Despite the moonlight, the night seemed darker than ever.

They dropped me off in the parking lot of the Granby Leader-Mail with barely a word. Ghost handed me a canvas bag. I reached in and pulled out a small revolver.

"If you want the ammunition, it will be buried in the weeds by the stop sign at the corner of Miltimore near where Booker killed Bakerstein," Ghost said. He wound up the window and drove away before I could say anything else. What would I have said anyways?

As the van pulled away I tried to see the licence plate number, but the plate light was out. Damn. I couldn't even tell what colour the thing was.

***

As the van pulled away Gorilla pulled off his mask and grunted as he shifted uncomfortably in the driver's seat, running his fingers through his curly black hair. Ghost pulled off his mask, adjusting the eye patch and wincing as he did so. The night's work was done.

29

Have you ever been asked to kill someone? Probably not. At least not seriously. Not seriously by a couple of men in masks who abduct you in the middle of the night and then stick a gun in your hands, telling you who killed your father.

I felt remarkably calm when I walked into the Granby Leader-Mail building, tossing the bag with the gun onto my desk. I sat down in the chair and reached into the sack. It was a .32 calibre revolver that looked a lot like the ones the kids played cowboys with. Not very big, like the long-barreled .38 Booker used on Tony Bakerstein, but I could tell by its weight, this was no kiddie toy.

That was the first wave of realization of what I was being asked to do, and the calmness evaporated. I stuffed it back in the canvas and carefully placed it in the desk drawer. Then I took it out, looked at it again, then put it away. Glancing over my shoulder, as if someone might be watching.

Kill someone? The whole idea seemed so odd, so foreign to my way of thinking. Sure, I'd been in a few fights as a kid, been angry with people from time to time, but this was just beyond my understanding. I'd never fired a gun before, and wasn't even sure I'd know how to load the damned thing. I nearly dropped it after pulling on a slide pin and the cylinder popped open. Damn. Now I knew how to load it. It felt more real than ever.

The shock of it all was starting to wear off, and the gravity of what the ghost and the gorilla said was starting to sink in. Stubby Booker had taken my dad from me. A dad I barely knew. Then again, do kids ever truly know their parents? Maybe if he had been around a little longer I would have known him, but that part of my life had been stolen. I would never know. I had built an entire person out of a few memories, and now I wasn't so sure if that person was real or not. Yet despite all of that, he remains a central figure in my life.

Sleep was out of the question. The rest of the night was spent alternating waves of sheer terror and absolute rage. Terror at the prospect of what had happened to me, and what was likely going to happen to me if I chose to do nothing. Rage at the people who had dragged me into this when all I really wanted to do was write news stories at this crappy little paper until I could get a better job in Montreal or Toronto. Rage at

Stubby Booker for making a mess of my life and having the gall to be angry at me about it.

It didn't take me long to figure out that I was going to have to keep this to myself, at least until I figured things out. A few folks already knew I was on the outs with Stubby, but probably not enough to connect me to him if he suddenly wound up dead. But if I so much as breathed a word of this to anyone the shit would hit the fan. Jen would be done with me if I even suggested the thought of killing Booker. Who would blame her? She didn't sign on to marry a murderer. Bankroft and my colleagues at the Leader-Mail would freak out, justifiably, and probably want me to go straight to the cops. Like that would do any good.

Then I started tossing scenarios around in my head. Gun battles where I emerged unscathed and stood over Booker's broken and bleeding body. Justice. Anger fully vented. He had it coming, the greasy little bastard. The chance to scream my rage into his dying face as the blood left his body.

And with it, a twinge of nausea. Followed by the feeling that I was hitchhiking on the road to hell. Chained into the driver's seat, more like it. Whatever I did, I couldn't see a nice outcome. No peace at the end, no happy ending, no getting my father back. Justice, but a justice where I would have to beg God for forgiveness every day for the rest of my life, and everything would be forever changed.

I got up and went over to the print manager's desk. I'd heard he kept a bottle in there, and I needed a drink. It was gin. I hate gin. But I took a swig anyways. Then I poured some into a coffee cup and put the bottle away. Once the cup was empty I went back to fill it again. And one more time for good measure. In between I paced the building, jumping every time the furnace kicked on, or the building shifted uncomfortably in the cold night air.

As the gin soaked in the nausea and fear subsided. I was just pissed off angry. Not just at Booker, but at the whole situation. Even if I did decide to shoot this guy, how in hell was I going to do it? I barely knew what he looked like, and I had no idea of how to make sure he didn't have his henchmen with him. Do I ambush him at his home? Draw him out for an open-air gunfight?

Ridiculous. Even drunk I knew that wasn't going to fly.

I took out the pistol again. The serial numbers had been filed off.

I'd heard of that watching Dragnet. It had a little bit of surface rust on it, but seemed to be in working order. I snapped the cylinder open and closed a few times, letting my drunk numb fingers get a feel for it. I lined up the sights on a picture on the wall of the local Member of Parliament and snapped off a few pretend rounds. Click. Click. Gee, that's not so hard.

Hell, I thought. If I'm even going to consider this, I should know if the damned thing even works. Besides, even if I didn't shoot him I could really use this to defend myself from those assholes who picked me up earlier. Or whoever was going to come after me next. There seemed to be a lineup. One way or another I was probably going to have to know how to use it.

With that in mind I put on my jean jacket, stuffing the pistol into the big inner pocket where I usually kept my notepad. I caught the edge of my desk with my hip on the way by, which spun me around. Oh yeah, my keys.

It took a fair bit of attention to guide the Falcon across the Mountain St. bridge and up Denison to Pierre Laporte. The sun was just starting to brighten the eastern horizon, but it was still pretty much dark. I felt safer in the dark.

The stop sign at the corner of Miltimore was easy enough to find. From there I could hear the brook where they found Tony Bakerstein. I tried to ignore it while I dug through a year's accumulation of weeds and grass at the base of the stop sign, but it kept pushing back into my mind. Poor hippie bastard. Just trying to make ends meet. It's not like he had a lot of options. Just like me. Now his kid didn't have a father anymore. Just like me. My mind was a non-stop litany of profanity. Fuck. Shit.

My hand came up against a plastic bag, and at first I pulled away. Then I reached in again, pulling the bag out. As expected, a plain brown box of .32 calibre bullets was inside. I stuffed it into my coat with the revolver and headed for the car. Despite the gin it was still bloody cold out.

Shivering in the cold and feeling a heady rush of fear, I fumbled the box open and snapped open the cylinder on the revolver. It's no easy thing to load a gun with shaking fingers and a head full of gin, but I got it done.

Stepping back out of the car and looking around, I pointed the pistol at a shrub about 20 feet away with both hands, pulling the hammer back like I'd seen them do in the movies. I barely touched the trigger before it barked into the dawn, jumping in my hand like it had a mind of its own.

"Jesus!" I said out loud, though I couldn't hear it above the ringing in my ears. I scrambled back to the car. It might not have been a very big handgun, but it sure scared the hell out of me.

The gin had pretty much burned out of my system for the trip back to the office. It was daylight, and like a vampire, I didn't want to be exposed in the light. I could feel danger everywhere and just wanted to go hide in a hole until... well, until this all went away. Which didn't seem like it was going to anytime soon. Fuck.

Back at the office I helped myself to another coffee cup of gin. I tucked the pistol and the box of bullets into the back of the desk drawer. It was going on 7 a.m. and the first people would be showing up for work in an hour. The last thing they needed to see was the homeless reporter playing with a handgun and stinking of gin.

When Linda did come in a few minutes after eight, she did see the homeless reporter, fully clothed, asleep on the couch, stinking of gin and sweat. She threw a blanket over me and let me sleep a bit longer.

***

When I came to it was a little after 9, and my head felt like it had spent the night in a vice. The same vice that squeezed all the moisture out of my mouth, leaving a not-so-gentle hint of cedar bark. That's why I don't like gin.

I put on a slightly dazed expression and headed past the advertizing department to the bathroom. The hot water was working, which was a good sign, and I splashed it on my face, trying to peel off the waxy layer of ether, sweat and gin that had accumulated there since the day before. With a little work and a fresh shirt I managed to look somewhat normal, even if I felt anything but that on the inside. Between the stress of figuring out how, or if, I was going to be able to avenge my father's murder, and a hammering hangover, it was going to be a rough day.

I went back to my desk, stopping by the coffee pot to tank up. Fidgeting with some papers I looked at the day ahead and realized it was going to be almost impossible to act like nothing had happened. But that was what I had to do, so I'd have to draw on my ability to keep looking calm.

Waiting for an opportune moment when no one seemed to be looking, I fished the plastic bag out of the trash and used it to reach into the back of the desk drawer to fetch the pistol. If anyone did see anything they'd just see me pulling something in a bag out of the drawer and stuffing it in my coat pocket.

"Going out to get some real coffee," I said to Linda quickly as I walked out.

It was overcast, with the feeling of snow in the air. I felt exposed, like a gopher that just came out of his hole and could smell a dog somewhere, but couldn't see it. No danger in sight, but it all seemed so menacing.

What I really wanted was to go someplace safe. But since that seemed out of the question perhaps someplace where I could be alone to try to get my head around the situation. Maybe get to know this gun a little better so at the very least I could protect myself. Or avoid shooting myself.

Ridiculous. And yet deadly serious. What in hell was I getting myself into?

I found myself heading along the Adamsville Road, with no particular place in mind. I saw a blue Valiant and my heart jumped. The old man in a fedora driving it didn't seem to notice me. My heart jumped again when a deer hunter stepped out of the woods onto the roadside, rifle in hand.

I passed through Adamsville and wound my way into East Farnham, turning right on Hall St. I realized I was making my way back to Brigham, and the burned out house I had recently called home. That wouldn't do. I couldn't bear to look at it. Pulling up next to the sand pit just outside the village, I turned the Falcon in. An empty sand pit was as good a place as any for a little target practice.

Shutting down the engine I got out and looked cautiously around. No one in sight. Good. I pulled the pistol out of my coat pocket, digging it out of the bag. Then I looked around for a target. A sand pile seemed good enough.

This time I was ready for the kick of the pistol when it let go. A puff of sand kicked up, the bullet disappearing into the heart of the pile. My ears still rang, but I wasn't nearly as scared as I had been. Shots two and three were more of the same.

Now I was ready to aim, and chose a clump of sod on the sand pile as my target. The first shot was pretty close, but still not on target. The next was well to the left of the mark. I missed again on the next shot. I pulled the trigger again. Nothing. Oh, time to reload.

Through it all I felt my nerves setting down. I still felt hungover, but I wasn't panicking anymore. I was mad. I was powerful. If I could handle this thing, I could make everything right. It was like having a really big friend to protect me. Holding the revolver with my right hand and resting it on my left palm I closed my left eye, took aim with the right, cocked the hammer and gently squeezed the trigger. It barked and the sod jumped.

The next dozen shots were more of the same, my nerves settling as I got familiar with the handgun. I even discovered the safety, after accidentally firing it while fiddling with it. Good thing it was unloaded. Damn these things are dangerous if you're not careful. I also came to the conclusion that tucking it into the waistband of my pants, like they did on TV, was a really good way to shoot off tender bits of my wedding tackle. No thanks.

By then I had settled into what I can only describe as a sense of detachment. I wasn't thinking about consequences. I wasn't thinking about what it actually means to kill another human being. Stubby Booker was a target, and if I hit that target I could get my life back. Boom. Bad man go away. My dad would be proud. My dad would be avenged and I could get on with my life.

Or, if I didn't get it right I could go to jail, lose my wife, and pretty much say goodbye to everything I had known. But in that moment those grim prospects didn't seem so menacing. Crossing that line seemed like the cold, logical choice.

A sense of fear returned when I realized I only had five bullets left. I'd better swing by Turcotte's gun shop on the way back to the office. And the liquor store.

By the time I got back to the office it was pushing noon.

"That was one long coffee," Linda said.

"Just what I needed," I said.

I left my coat on for the afternoon as I worked at my desk. A call to Fernand Dubois gave me a short story on a car crash just outside

Adamsville. The MP had also sent out a press release about additional funding for some repair work on Route 139 between Cowansville and Granby. The road was only a few years old and it already needed some fresh asphalt.

While my outside world seemed to return to normal, inside I wanted to get the day over with. I had some planning to do.

30

Informant ties Stubby Booker multiple murders

By Dave Rogers

Granby Leader-Mail Staff Reporter

GRANBY – Notorious Roxton businessman Sanford "Stubby" Booker has been linked to no fewer than three murders, including that of a police officer believed to have been killed nearly 25 years ago.

The accuser – who remains in hiding pending an eventual criminal trial – spoke to the Leader-Mail on condition of anonymity. A former associate of Booker's, the man says he has the factual evidence police need to put Booker away for the murder of Quebec Police Force officer Richard McConnell in 1951. The man also alleges Booker's involvement in the murder of the only witness to that crime, Dave Rogers Sr., and in the murder of Anthony Bakerstein this summer.

"I have been working on this for a long time, and now I know everything the police will need to put him away," the source said. "He is a bad man, and he will pay a very heavy price."

Booker has a long history of run-ins with the law, but has for the most part remained unscathed. According to court records he served a two-year sentence for obstruction of justice in the McConnell case. McConnell's body was never found, so murder charges were never laid. Booker did however serve time for obstruction of justice.

The accuser claims to have a detailed knowledge of the man's business dealings. He says Booker's criminal dealings go far beyond the murders, including stolen goods and drug smuggling. His evidence will be taken to the QPF within the next few days, he says.

Of course, I knew that this story wasn't ever going to be published. For one thing, mister "associate" didn't even exist as far as I knew. But I figured it would make Booker look over his shoulder, which meant less attention on me. I had been paranoid long enough, now it was his turn.

But I was pretty sure Stubby wouldn't be able to figure that out. The paper's reputation as the "Granby Liar" meant it wouldn't be too much of a stretch to think it would publish a story based on nothing more than anonymous allegations. Judging from what I had heard of the previous lawsuits, not much of a stretch at all.

Then came the note:

"Stubby: You and I have to meet. Sealed copies of this story are in the hands of one of my colleagues, and also a reporter at the Montreal Star. If anything happens to me they will publish the story and will also have the necessary background information to take to the police. They will know where I am and who I am meeting.

Meet me at the pit on the Sand Road in Brigham tomorrow evening at 7 p.m. Come alone. Unarmed. If you don't show up my informant will go to the police and this story will be published in the Leader-Mail and the Star, and you will be arrested."

It wasn't all lies. But then again, isn't all bait just a smattering of truth that covers a bitter reality? Let him chew on that for awhile.

***

Stubby Booker lived alone. He preferred it that way. He always said he could only live with someone he trusted. Stubby valued his independence, and besides, he liked to use his alone time to scheme and plan. If he wanted company he'd bring in one of the dogs from the yard.

Tonight the dogs were all outside, and wasted no time in letting him know when the car pulled up in front of his mailbox. He clicked off the TV, standing in his darkened living room so he couldn't be seen as he watched the car pull up to the box, just past the glow of the yard light. He cursed softly, realizing he couldn't make out what kind of car it was, or who was inside.

As the car pulled away the driver leaned on the horn, its leaky muffler adding to the chorus as it rattled off into the distance. Whoever it was, they wanted to get his attention. They had it.

Stubby had been shot at before, and the memory kept him cautious. An 11 p.m. mail delivery was out of character, and it set off the radar that had kept him alive and angry for so many years. The dogs, all three of them, felt it too, barking and snapping at the cool night air and the mystery deliveryman.

Slipping on his work boots and pulling a sawed-off shotgun out from behind a panel in the back of the coat closet he exited through the back of the house. Rather than walk directly to the mailbox he cut around the back of the house, past a pile of pallets and through the ditch. He stopped in the ditch for a couple of minutes, listening for sounds and staring into the blackness below him so his eyes could adjust to the dark as much as possible. The dogs had relaxed, and with the exception of a distant truck, there was little to be heard.

He cut across the road, then worked his way up the far ditch, stopping opposite the postal box. Reasonably sure there wasn't anyone around, he eased up out of the ditch and crossed the road. A final listen to the mailbox (he heard nothing) and he opened it up, reaching in and pulling out the brown manila envelope. Feeling nothing hard inside, he decided to wait until he got inside to open it. Too cold. Looking around he saw nothing, so he walked straight back to the house.

Boots off, Stubby settled at the kitchen table and tore off the end of the envelope. He pulled out the four sheets of plain white paper, reading the news story first, then the note. He stared at it blankly for a few minutes, letting the information sink in.

"So, Rogers is out for vengeance," he muttered to himself. "Why is this little shithead being such a pain in the ass?"

Three murders. Rogers had tied him to three murders, including the death of his father. What bullshit, he thought. There's no way any of this could be proven, even with a well-placed anonymous source.

The secret witness business was still cause for concern: If this person did exist, who would it be? Stubby had worked hard to recruit the right people, weeding out the petty thugs and the yahoos who thought they were bigger and tougher than they really were. He knew how to show them how small they really were. Stubby was proud of those who populated his inner circle, people who could be trusted.

Even then he made sure none of them knew the whole story. Each one of his top people were sworn to only talk about work at work, and were only told what they needed to know. Their wives didn't even know the details of their daily work lives.

His mind filed through the people who worked for him, but no one stood out. But you could never be absolutely sure of anyone, except yourself. And for a lot of people even that was a stretch.

Maybe someone had connected the dots. Some of the dots. And chances were some of it was based on rumours that circulated in small towns. If you believed the rumours, Stubby had killed as many as a dozen people. Such bullshit. But it kept people afraid of him, and that's the way he liked it. If someone thinks you'll beat them up they may still come after you. If they think you just might kill them they'll leave you alone.

"So what's he going to do?" Stubby thought to himself. "Looks like he wants to get even."

It smelled like an ambush. An ambush by an amateur, motivated by sheer anger. Stubby knew about anger. He also knew about control. Good luck, kid.

31

I was kind of on autopilot all day. It was Thursday, deadline day. I didn't have quite as many stories as usual, but Bankroft left me alone. Bad form to pick on the homeless guy about his productivity.

Still, I did manage to bang something out on a proposed project to expand the emergency department of the hospital in Cowansville, and I rewrote a press release from the union representing the textile workers at Esmond Mills calling for better safety practices.

But my mind was elsewhere, frantically going over the details of what lay ahead, trying to make sure all of my bases were covered. My plan was pretty simple: Lure Booker into the sand pit, shoot, shovel and shut up.

Mostly I was just wishing the whole thing would go away. The desire to pack up and run fought with the desire to get even, treading on my brain as they did so. A few times I found myself headed for the bathroom, where I would try to catch my breath and look at the stranger in the mirror.

My God, what was going to happen to me? What in Hell did I think I was doing?

I only left the office once, and I made sure I had my gun with me. It was like having a big friend along. All that for a trip to the store for a bag of chips. The only thing I ate all day.

Have you ever gone into a bar and you can feel like the whole place is about to erupt into a brawl? My whole universe was a tinder box. That at any moment all Hell would break loose with no easy way out. The force of all that tension was drawing me to a sand pit on a back road, and into the vortex of events that is created when one man tries to kill another. A vortex that can drain the colour out of the world, just as it drains the colour from a man's face as he breathes his last.

I have often found that just when stress seems overwhelming, there's a part of me that shuts down. I'm not nervous anymore. I feel like shit, but I'm not about to lose it. That feeling settled in at about 5:30 p.m., right after I puked up the bag of chips. Salt and vinegar wasn't the best choice.

Washing my face in the sink I decided it was time to go.

"You're white as a sheet," Rachel said, breathing smoke out as she spoke. "The homeless life doesn't suit you."

"I just can't wait to sleep in a real bed," I said. "Going back to the city tomorrow for a shit, shave and a shampoo."

I wandered over to Harry's desk, doing my best to act casual.

"That's it for me," I said. "I'm heading out for awhile."

"What? The sun's barely gone down," Bankroft grumbled. "Besides, where are you going to go?"

"Just out. I've been cooped up in here all day," I said. "And I'll be back here later, so in the meantime I've got to go somewhere."

The best lies are the simplest ones. Harder to get tripped up.

"You'd better find yourself a place to live," Bankroft said. "That wife of yours won't take kindly to you living in an office for very long."

"Yeah, I know," I said noncommittally.

"You are planning to find a place to live, right?"

"Soon enough. I need a bit of time to get my head together."

"We're just getting you broken in, that's all. It's a pain in the ass having to train new people."

"Thanks, Harry." I knew that was about as close to praise as I was ever going to get from him.

Stepping out into the evening the bitter air caught my breath. It was still early November, but the mercury had already dropped several degrees below freezing. Well, at least there wasn't any snow yet. I grabbed a sweater out of the back seat and put it on, then put my jean jacket over the top. I was freezing cold before I left the building, and this weather wasn't helping.

The Falcon took a couple of minutes to warm up, and the windshield stubbornly refused to clear. Damn. No scraper. I used the edge of a piece of cardboard to peel the frost off the inside. Good enough.

I had plenty of time, but figured it wouldn't be a bad idea to get there early. Make sure everything was as it should be. I'd never been to a killing before, and I didn't want to be late. Sorry I'm late Mr. Booker, could we reschedule?

A wandering mind is a ridiculous thing sometimes.

On the Adamsville Road I came to the realization that driving through Brigham might not be the best thing. Since my house had been burned people were always watching. Better to come in by the back way so no one would be able to place my car anywhere near the area.

Coasting in to East Farnham I pulled in to the yard at DuChene's, staying well away from the other parked cars. The scare I'd had there a few short months ago seemed distant, like it belonged to another life. I took a second to check the pistol, make sure it was loaded and the safety on. I dumped the rest of the box of shells onto a side pocket. I'd feel like an idiot if I ran out of ammo. A soon-to-be-dead idiot. But all I wanted was one shot. One clean shot and it would be over.

What was I doing? The voice in my head said it was time to run away. Just take off and head for who-knows-where, stopping by NDG to pick up Jen. Simple. Safe. No killing.

But it wasn't so simple. It wasn't so safe. And it just wasn't right. The cool resolve returned, and I pried my hands off the steering wheel. Keep your nerve, stick to the plan, and get it done.

I had a flashlight with me, but I wasn't planning to use it. While a light might be good for spotting someone, it's also a great way to attract attention to yourself. I double-checked it as well, stuffing it into my left hand pocket.

The headlights cast a yellowish glow on the sand as I entered the pit. I drove for a hundred yards or so, then pulled up behind a dune. I killed the motor, shut the lights off and used the flashlight to check the time: 6:40.

Stepping out of the car I couldn't help but notice how dark it was. Cold and dark and quiet. I wished it would stay that way. That my plan would stay tucked away in the darkness, never to be used.

***

Stubby watched as the car pulled in. Hard to tell, but it sure looked like the one that had visited his mailbox last night. The tail lights looked right. Sitting on a rock pile he hunched down, watching the car approach. It came straight towards him before veering to the left and parking.

Stubby Booker wasn't going to be ambushed by some kid. He knew better than that. That's why he'd come early to get the lay of the land. It also gave him a chance to be sure Rogers hadn't brought anyone along with him. When the car door opened and the dome light went on he could tell Rogers was alone.

"He's got balls," Booker thought. Most people would have turned tail and run. Not even showed up. "Balls as big as his dad's."

Still showing up was one thing. Shooting someone was another entirely. Paper targets and tin cans are one thing, a living being is another. Most people can't do it. Stubby got over it a long time ago.

Stubby also knew that the key here was to keep Rogers rattled. He'd been to meetings like this before, so he knew what to do. A roll of wire, a sealed beam and a car battery were a good start. He flipped a switch and 50 feet to his right a pair of lights bathed the Ford Falcon in light. Rogers scrambled to the far side of the car, hiding behind it. Right where Stubby could see him. Or at least enough of him to know he was scared. And armed, judging by the glint of metal in the kid's right hand.

***

I hadn't expected lights. To be honest I didn't know what to expect. And when they came on they scared the beJesus out of me. Lights, but not a word. I scrambled behind the car, the only thought in my mind being that being in the light made me a perfect target. Not only was I visible, but I couldn't see a damned thing other than those lights. When they snapped off all I could see were a pair of glowing purple orbs in a sea of black.

Shit. Shit, shit, shit. Already this was not working out like I planned.

***

Stubby sat in the darkness for a couple of minutes, not saying anything. Then he flipped the switch again, bathing the car in light. He kept quiet, letting the lights work their way into Dave's mind. Keep him scared.

"Do you have any idea what you're trying to do?" he called out to the man hunched down next to the car. Stubby saw the head jerk to the side. Rogers had expected the voice to come from where the lights were.

"I know what I have to do," came the reply. Remarkably calm sounding for a man hiding behind a parked car, Booker thought.

"And just what is it that you have to do?"

"You know damn well what I have to do."

"Well, judging from that bullshit story you sent me, I'm thinking you want to get even for me killing your old man."

"Among other things."

"There's just a few problems with that, starting with the fact that I have no intention of getting hit with that pea shooter of yours. You even know how to fire that thing?"

"Well enough to take care of you."

"Well, here's another problem for you to consider, boy. For starters, that bit you wrote about me having your dad killed, it's bullshit."

"What?" the voice called back.

"It's bullshit. I never could have killed your old man."

"Why not? Didn't you go to jail because of him?"

"Yeah. But I didn't kill him."

***

I could hear blood pounding in my ears. I felt dizzy. Mostly, I was intensely confused.

"What in hell do you mean?"

"Okay boy, you wanna talk, or do you wanna shoot? Shoot at me and you'll die. Put your gun on the hood of the car and we'll have a chat."

The way I saw it, standing in the glare of the lights, I was pretty much screwed either way. I put the pistol on the hood, but not too far away, just in case.

I could hear workboots in brambles, the faint rattle of gravel. Then a short man with one really thick eyebrow merged into the light. Stubby Booker in the flesh. Cleaner than when I saw him in the restaurant. Older than he looked in the pictures I'd seen.

I didn't even know what to say. I just stared at him while my brain tried to grasp what he had just said. The desire to make it all go away returned with a vengeance. I waited for him to start talking.

"Your dad and I went way back. Damn he was a funny son of a bitch. He got us into a few scrapes, but we always managed to walk between the raindrops," Booker said. "He just liked to have fun."

Stubby walked up and leaned on the hood of the car, reaching into his jacket to pull out a pack of Old Port cigars. He tapped the cigar on the hood before lighting it with a wooden match, dragged across the corroded chrome of my rear view mirror.

"Your dad ratted me out. Because of him I went to jail. I wanted him dead. But this was Dave, 'Slippers' we used to call him. I was his Best Man at his wedding. Did you know that?"

I hadn't.

"I got him alone once after he went to the cops, but I just couldn't do it. We'd grown apart, but we were still the best of friends. He had his life, I had mine. I slapped him around, told him what an asshole he was. But when it came time to pull the trigger, I couldn't do it."

He paused for a minute, as if considering what he was going to say next. I stayed quiet. Hell, I didn't know what to say anyway.

"I cut him lose. But I told him if I ever saw him again, I'd kill him. I told him to pack up his family and leave. Or else. I never saw or heard from him again. I found out he was dead when they let me out of jail."

"So what happened to him, then?"

"It was an accident. All those years of him swinging off of ladders and silos and rooftops, and he zigs when he should have zagged on a girder. Nothing more to it than that."

"But why in hell have you been harassing me. Sending your goons to beat up my wife and burn down my house?"

"Kid, I have no idea what you're talking about."

"But... whaa?" I was starting to lose it. I took a second to breathe. My chest was tight, and it felt like I hadn't breathed in awhile. The air was sharp, and it stung my lungs. Somehow I knew he wasn't lying, which raised more questions than it answered.

"The notes, the two guys who attacked my wife and then came back to burn down my house. All of it. It has to be you."

"Rogers, let's be clear. Your old man betrayed me. But I didn't kill him.

I don't like you because of what your dad did to me. When I saw your name in the paper I was pissed. But what the hell good would it do me? I'm not full of piss and vinegar like I was back then. Kill you? Just too damned complicated and I can't be bothered. Hell, if I killed everyone I didn't like, it would be pretty damned quiet around here."

Lighting another match he hunched forward to relight the Old Port. As he did so a bullet tore through the night air.

32

I stood there like an idiot, stunned by the sound of the shot and the metallic clank as the bullet slammed into the passenger fender. Stubby reached over and pushed me backwards, stumbling into the shadow behind the car. He was practically on top of me.

I couldn't figure out where the shot had come from, but Stubby seemed to figure it out pretty quickly. Hunched by the driver's side fender, he made a quick grab for my .32 on the hood. As he did a second shot rang out, the bullet punching in the hood before tumbling up into the night sky.

"Stay the fuck down!" Stubby said, as if I'd do anything different.

Booker crawled on his hands and knees to the rear of the car, then veered right, into the darkness. A minute ago I was getting ready to kill him, and now it felt like he was abandoning me. I had no idea where he was, or if he'd left me for whoever it was doing the shooting.

Shit, he's got my gun. Abandoned, alone, unarmed, with at least two armed and ready people in my immediate vicinity. This was not at all going like I'd planned. I was supposed to be calmly digging a grave by now.

Shot number three came through the passenger window and punched a hole in the driver's door, coming out about two feet from my head. Shit! Shit! Shit! What in hell was I supposed to do now?

I decided to crawl towards the back of the car, figuring that since the shots were all hitting the front that maybe that would put more car between me and the shooter. Crawling under the rear of the car I tried to look out into the light without being seen. Then I realized that I was lying right under the gas tank. I felt like there was a bomb over my head. I could feel the hair on my neck reaching up to greet it.

I couldn't see anything beyond the glare of the sealed beams, but by now had at least figured out where the shooting was coming from. I decided the best thing to do was make like Stubby and crawl off into the night away from the shooter, and hope he couldn't see in the dark.

I was just getting ready to start shifting my body backwards when one of the sealed beams changed direction, coming to rest on a sand dune I hadn't seen when I pulled in. Almost instantly I heard shots. Lots of shots. Six loud, deep shots a row, followed by a pause and then four more, smaller shots. My .32 was being put to use. The sound bouncing off the surrounding hills before blending into the night.

Then silence. Nothing. The spot lights went off. All I could hear was the ringing in my ears and the sound of my own rapid, shallow breathing. Sweat trickled down the back of my neck. Gas tank or not, I didn't dare move.

I thought I heard a rustling to my right. Then the sound of boots running on gravel. A sealed beam came on from the top of the dune that had been in the light a moment earlier.

"Move and you're dead," Booker was saying. There were some sounds followed by groans. "Get up, you fucker!" Booker's voice echoed almost as much as the gunshots had.

A low moan in reply, followed by more rustling sounds. More sounds, I think it was Stubby continuing to put the boots to the shooter. The sealed beam fell to the gravel, splaying its light down the side of the dune.

"Move and you're dead," Booker repeated, this time the tone had softened, but lost none of its authority. The light was picked up again.

I saw the man getting up, bathed in the light of the sealed beam. He began to stumble down the dune, heading towards the car. He stopped at one point and I saw the sealed beam come up and then sharply down. When the light was on him again he lay face down in the sand.

"Rogers, get out here," Booker said sharply. "Take the light."

I crawled out from under the car, sand sticking to the sweat on my face. I put on my best calm look and tried to walk casually over, as if this was all normal. But my legs felt like I was walking on stilts. Stubby handed me the light.

With the light on our shooter, Stubby hooked a hand through the man's belt. Booker wasn't very big, but he had no trouble lifting our shooter and throwing him over the over the hood of my car. Just to make a point he then pumped a fist into his kidney.

"You fucker! How dare you try to shoot me!" he yelled, punching him again. He rolled him over and there he was, a one-eyed sniper with a hooked nose that was gushing blood. The eye patch looked like a hole in his head in the dim light.

"Time for some answers," Booker said.

"Go fuck yourself," came the reply.

"Wrong answer," came the swift reply, followed by a fist to the stomach. The man bent double and fell off the car onto the ground. Stubby grabbed him by the hair, sticking his face in close next to the man's. I could see sweat pouring off Stubby's face, and an expression of pure, terrifying rage.

"This is only going to get worse, you little bastard," he said quietly.

In that moment I understood why everyone was so afraid of Stubby Booker. There was a ferocity mixed with a coldness of spirit. Rage harnessed for a purpose. Rage without remorse. This wasn't going to end well. But it was going to end exactly the way Stubby wanted it to.

I still dream about the next ten minutes. The cigar burns. The yelling. The dislocated elbow. The repeated blows to the ribs, face and anything else that came into range. The screams of agony that still wake me in the night.

"Okay, just stop," the man said through a muffled mass of blood and teeth as he lay on the ground. "Frank McConnell."

Stubby stood still.

"What was that?"

"Frank McConnell. I think you know who we're talking about," he said. There was a defiant tone in his voice. "Or do you not even remember the name of the cop you killed?"

For a moment no one moved. I could hear the blood pounding in my ears. And the high hiss of silence fraught with tension.

"What's that to you?"

"I worked with him."

"Shit, this guy's a cop?" I said, losing whatever semblance of cool I had. Visions of going to jail loomed in my head. If I was out of my league in planning to shoot Stubby Booker, I was way out of my league now.

"Not anymore," Booker said. "I remember you. You and that other prick who decided to beat the hell out of me. Lost your jobs over that, didn't you?

Silence from the bloody body that knelt on the ground next to the car.

"So, Mr. Farstall. Now I remember you. What happened to that eye?"

"His fucking wife gouged it out."

"My wife? You attacked my wife? You're the bastard that burned down my house?" I was completely bewildered, the rage boiling deep but not yet brought to the surface. "You fuck!"

I kicked him half-heartedly. Then again. Then I got mad. I could feel his ribs give way as I kicked harder, and it felt good. I was finally able to vent some rage on someone.

The next thing I knew Stubby was hauling me off Farstall. Damn he was strong for a little guy.

"Relax. Leave this to me."

"So where's your buddy?" Booker asked, turning his attention to Farstall. "Where's Burson? Is he here with you?"

"He's not with us," Farstall replied.

"Who in hell is us?" Booker said.

"You'll find out soon enough."

I immediately dropped into a crouch, expecting more shots at any second. Booker loosened his grip on Farstall, dropping down next to the fender and shutting the sealed beam off.

"Lionel, help me, I've been shot!" Farstall cried out.

Silence in return. We waited for what felt like an incredibly long time. Nothing. "Lionel... Come on... he got me in the leg..." Farstall's voice trailed off. The waiting continued, me waiting to see what unfolded next and Stubby, apparently, sizing up the situation, though I couldn't see his face.

"Hear that?" Stubby said.

In the distance we heard the sound of a car starting somewhere at the back of the pit. The engine revved high as we saw the glare of headlights behind a mountain range made of sand. We ducked behind the trunk of the car, Stubby rummaging his pockets and reloading his .38. The lights got closer, the engine more frantic.

Just as the lights were about to loom into view they veered to the left, onto the road and off into the night. The sound of car wheels digging for traction on a gravel road joined the deep yet frantic rumble of a V-8 engine. As the sound subsided, so did Farstall's hope of rescue.

Stubby put the sealed beam back on, shining it directly into Farstall's face. There were tears on the man's cheeks, mixing with blood. Through the cuts and bruises his face bore the look of utter defeat. The look of a man who, despite giving it his best effort, had failed at his life's mission. Failed and abandoned. The die was cast and he had lost.

Booker wasted no time, grabbing me by the collar of my jacket and hauling me around the other side of the Falcon. He held onto my collar, and my undivided attention.

"Here's what you are going to do," he said. "Tomorrow, first thing, you're going to take this shitbox of a car over to Homer Valliere's scrap yard on Fordyce. He'll give you a hundred bucks for it, with no questions asked about the bullet holes. Then you get your ass back to Montreal and sit there and don't say a fucking thing. On Monday, come back to work and act like nothing's happened."

He paused, then twisted my collar a little more tightly.

"The thing to remember here is that if you talk, we both get arrested. If you get arrested and rat me out, you won't live to see the inside of a jail cell. Now get the fuck outta here."

He let go of my collar, and like a robot I walked over to the car and opened the door. The seat was covered in glass particles. I swept them off with my hand, sat down and cranked the engine over. It coughed once, then came to life.

"Uh, where's my gun?" I asked, leaning my head out the window.

"You won't need it. I'll take care of it."

I dropped it into Drive, and slowly pulled away, leaving Booker and Farstall in the sand. My mind was blank, focused only on driving, with so many other thoughts in my mind that they pushed each other aside, wiping the slate clean.

Just as I pulled onto the road the sound of a single shot rang out, the sound hitting me like a slap in the back of the head.

Stubby turned away, not wanting to watch the death throes. He had to keep his eye on the big picture. He had a septic tank to find.

33

I spent the next couple of hours driving around, trying to figure out what to do. It was damned cold driving with no passenger window, but it took me awhile to notice. Occasionally I passed under a streetlight, the punched in hood with the blood smear coming into sharp relief.

Shit, I have to get rid of this car, I realized. But bringing it to a scrap yard with blood all over it was not a good idea, even if Stubby said Homer Vallieres wouldn't say anything. By the time I pulled over to try to wipe it off the blood had congealed and stuck like varnish. Frozen ditch water and a rag didn't help in the attempt.

So here I was. Attempted murder. Accessory to murder. Accessory to torture. Tampering with evidence. Assault. Possession of a restricted firearm. The more I sat there the more charges, real or otherwise, I came up with. A long stay in jail was becoming a real possibility.

Many other real possibilities were fighting with less likely but no less scary scenarios: Farstall's sidekick took off, and God knows where he was, or what he was planning to do. What about Stubby? What would the cops be thinking?

Then there were all of the other realizations: That my father had not in fact been murdered; that I had been set up to kill someone, and had actually tried to do it; that the guy who I thought had been trying to kill me had in fact just saved my life.

And by going along to save my own skin, I had basically made a deal with a very bad man. A guy who was at his core much worse than Farstall and his cowardly friend who had beat up my wife and burned down my house.

My wife. Jen. Damn. How in hell was I going to explain this one?

I stuck to the back roads, looking for a place to lie low. It was Bull Pond Road when I was in Cowansville, but turned into Cleveland when I crossed into Iron Hill. A right on Sanborn and another on Chapman and I was on Centre. Shit. A few miles down the road Centre turned into the Sand Road. I was driving in circles.

I found an entry into a field lined with stone walls. I cranked the heater up and let the engine idle for a few minutes, getting out as much heat as I could. Then I shut it down and settled in to try to get some sleep.

What little sleep I did get was fitful, filled with chaotic dreams, images of what I had just seen while my father looked on. But he looked different than I remembered. Emotions brought to the fore that I had never seen in him before. In my dreams I was trying to ask him questions, but the words wouldn't come. He remained silent and then, despite my pleading, turned away. I was on my own.

I gave up on sleeping as the sun started to paint the first shades of blue on the eastern sky. I was cold, damp and tired. The frosted timothy crackled under my feet as I walked to the stone wall to take a leak. On the way back I walked around back and fished a wrench out of the trunk. I left the bloody and beaten hood of the Falcon in an outcrop of brush that had grown up around a disorderly section of the stone wall.

In the end I didn't have much other choice than to take Stubby's advice: I dumped the car at the scrap yard, headed for the city and on Monday was back at my desk acting like nothing ever happened. Telling everyone that my rusty old Falcon had finally died wouldn't be much of a stretch. Jen could tell I was stressed, but given that our house had been burned, she'd been attacked and I had been sleeping on a couch at the office for the last couple of weeks, it seemed logical.

***

In the weeks and months that followed, my ability to look relatively calm when I was actually about to crap myself was put to the test time and again. Like when the ballistics report came back to say that Booker's gun wasn't the one used to shoot Tony Bakerstein. It wasn't even the same caliber: Bakerstein was shot with a .38, not a .32. Likely the one I had been given by my masked abductors.

Or when Fernand Dubois phoned to say they'd arrested Lionel Baudelaire for the arson on my house. Or when they brought me in for questioning after Baudelaire tried to implicate Stubby and me in the death of his buddy, Reggie Farstall. He even managed to convince the cops to carry out a search warrant at Homer's scrapyard, but the Falcon, bullet wounds and all, had already been fed into the crusher.

After a couple of weeks I found an apartment in Granby, just a couple of blocks from the paper. I even managed to beg and borrow $300, which I pooled with the scrapyard money for the Falcon to buy an elderly Vauxhall which, to be honest, was in worse shape than the Falcon.

Once Baudelaire was arrested I even managed to convince Jen to move back. My nightmares had calmed down by then. She didn't ask nearly as many questions as I thought she would, and for awhile at least, life returned to some semblance of normal. I suspect she chose to be silent, lest she hear something that couldn't be taken back.

And so it unfolded all around me. For a man who earned his living from telling stories, I learned the value of silence. I might always get the last word, but only if I wanted to.

At work I quietly tried to stay away from the police stories, content to read what my colleagues had learned by reading it in the paper like everyone else.

June 20, 1976.

By John McAuslan

GRANBY- Roxton businessman Sanford 'Stubby' Booker was convicted of obstruction of justice on Tuesday in the disappearance of former police officer Reginald Farstall.

Booker was however acquitted of charges that he supplied firearms and explosives to the People for an English-Speaking Quebec, or that he authorized a member of the vigilante group to set fire to the home of Raoul Castonguay in Brigham.

Ainsley Wright, a retired Lt. Colonel in the Canadian Army, is alreadyin jail awaiting sentencing for his role as the leader of PESQ. At a hearing last month Wright told a judge he had called for the group to be disbanded, and accepted full blame for its activities. He however denied ever ordering Castonguay's house to be burned.

The main witness against Booker was Lionel Baudelaire, who was himself arrested by police in connection with the burning of the home of Granby Leader-Mail reporter Dave Rogers in Brigham last November. Further investigation connected Baudelaire to the Castonguay fire, which he later also admitted to.

By his own admission Baudelaire had worked for Booker for two years, and joined PESQ at Booker's request. He claimed the Castonguay fire was ordered by Booker, something the Roxton businessman denied repeatedly during his trial.

Booker was primarily accused by Baudelaire of murdering former police officer Reginald Farstall at a sand pit in Brigham. However an extensive search of Booker's properties failed to turn up any evidence that the crime took place. Farstall remains missing.

Despite a number of run-ins with the law Booker has remained relatively unscathed over the years. Strangely, the only other jail time he ever served was over two decades ago, also for obstruction of justice in the disappearance of a police officer.

Booker was sentenced to two years less a day, to be served in a provincial jail.

While I managed to put up walls to protect myself from the outer world, my inner life was profoundly changed. By the violence. By my own desire for violence, for revenge. By the knowledge that my father wasn't who I had always believed him to be, and that I would never truly know him for who he was. He still visits me in my dreams, but never speaks. Never explains. Never asks for forgiveness.

THE END

CROSSFIELD
PUBLISHING

Printed in Great Britain
by Amazon

46298103R00116